VALLEY OF THE GUNS

Zack Clay is looking for a quiet life, but he hasn't reckoned on range-grabbers Dutch Haas and Burt Helidon bringing in sundry gunfighters to hassle him. Clay meets fists and boots with the same, gunsmoke with gunsmoke. In the end, they hang a badge on him. Then things really hot up in Benbow. But the hustlers, gunslingers, the wild trailmen and townsmen who put dollars before citizens all find that stubborn Zack Clay won't go down without a fight . . .

Books by Rick Dalmas
in the Linford Western Library:

SIX FOR LARAMIE
RENEGADE'S LEGACY
COUNT THE DEAD

RICK DALMAS

VALLEY OF THE GUNS

Complete and Unabridged

LINFORD
Leicester

First published in Great Britain in 2011 by
Robert Hale Limited
London

First Linford Edition
published 2012
by arrangement with
Robert Hale Limited
London

British Library CIP Data

Dalmas, Rick.
  Valley of the guns. - -
  (Linford western library)
  1. Western stories.
  2. Large type books.
  I. Title II. Series
  823.9'2–dc23

  ISBN 978–1–4448–1275–6

Published by
F. A. Thorpe (Publishing)
Anstey, Leicestershire

Set by Words & Graphics Ltd.
Anstey, Leicestershire
Printed and bound in Great Britain by
T. J. International Ltd., Padstow, Cornwall

1

The Avengers

Because he had had to shoot the horse out from under the escaping redhead, Zack's six-gun was empty now.

But the redhead was stumbling to his feet, groping for his own gun, dusty, bloody, shaken, and killing mad.

So Zack rode him down — spurred the sweating, snorting buckskin with a jab of the rowels that had the big horse leaping forward like an arrow shot from a longbow. The redhead went down to stay this time, the buckskin not happy with the heavy jerks on the reins and the muttered curses of the rider. The hoofs plunged and stomped and the killer died screaming.

Zack hauled rein, leaned forward to pat the sweaty neck hide, whispering in the laid-back ear, calming the animal.

He looked down at the man on the ground.

The naked, battered and bloody woman back at the ferry crossing had gasped '*He's — got — red hair*,' then died in Zack's arms.

Well, the hair was red now all right — *blood* red.

Chess skidded his sweaty, dust-streaked roan in beside Zack, grimaced, lifted his gaze to Zack's sober face.

'Never would've thought you'd be a man to do that.' When Zack didn't speak or move, not even his eyes, Chess lifted his hat to scratch his damp hair, and asked, 'You know her from somewhere?'

Then the clear brown eyes shifted to his face. 'No. What difference would that make? She and her two daughters were raped and murdered by Red and his pards. Someone had to square things. Her man couldn't do it.'

Chess nodded slowly, remembering the man's body they had found behind the ferry station, dangling by his twisted neck from a fork in a tree. He swallowed and gestured back to where Frank and Dodds were sitting their mounts, staring at the other two sprawled bodies near the remains of the campfire.

'We got all three of the bastards, anyway.'

Zack sighed and turned the settling buckskin slowly. 'Let's get back to the landing and bury the woman and her girls.' The brown eyes clouded suddenly. '*Girls*! One about twelve, the other mebbe five — *five*, for Chris'sakes!'

He gritted the last words and lifted his reloaded six-gun, but lowered it almost immediately; it was pointless wasting lead on men already dead. 'Let's go.'

'We gonna leave these fellers?'

Zack's face was cold. 'You want to lose sweat and energy burying this scum? I only hope they don't poison the animals that eat 'em. Come on.'

Chess's long face was pale and he frowned as he watched Zachariah Clay spur away.

Who would ever have thought that he

of all men would have relentlessly hunted down these killers and dished out the roughest kind of justice Chess had ever been a part of?

Back in the valley he was known as a quiet, unassuming man who worked mighty hard in his efforts to prove up on his quarter section straddling Bowleg Creek. He was a man who would settle imminent trouble with a few well-chosen words, but, at the same time, if he saw that violence was inevitable, then he would stand his ground. As far as Chess could recollect he had only seen Zack, as folk called him, in two fist fights, neither particularly bloody, but he won them quickly with bone-jarring blows. Afterwards, he picked up his opponent out of the dust and helped him into the nearest bar where he bought him a beer and a shot of whiskey.

Burt Helidon, likely the most powerful rancher in the valley, certainly the richest, had had no luck at all trying to persuade Zack to sell out to him. He offered a good, fair deal, too: stay put, prove up, then sell the quarter section to Helidon at a fine profit.

Zack's answer: 'Good offer, Mr Helidon, but if I sweat blood and crack muscles building this place up, I aim to keep it for myself.'

'Hell, man, you're a loner. What's it matter where you live? You got no wife to please or . . . '

About then, Burt realized he had said something he shouldn't have. He frowned, but backed off quickly, finishing somewhat lamely with:

'Well, let's leave it till you've got full title and we'll talk again.'

Zack hadn't made any comment one way or another at the suggestion and Helidon rode his Arab grey back to his own range much more roughly than he had intended.

That was the kind of man Chess knew Zack to be. Tough when he had to be; stubborn, too, kept to himself but he was a good boss, had hired Chess, Frank and Dodds to help him drive the

5

small herd of mavericks he had rounded up in the hills and marked with his Circle Z brand to the railhead market at Two Peaks.

'Got no cash, boys,' Zack had told them openly. 'You drive 'em to market with me, you get fed and share half of what I sell 'em for. Beef prices aren't too high right now, but you'll do all right.'

They sealed the deal over a few beers.

Now, after they had buried the woman and her family at the ferry landing, Zack walked to the small rise that overlooked the river. It had dropped a few feet since the flash flood, but the waters still raged and surged, tearing away part of the banks even as they watched.

Trouble was, the river had broken its banks while they were hunting down the killers. It had flooded through the small pasture with its sapling fences where the ferryman let drovers leave their herds while he ferried them across river a few at a time on his barge.

Now the barge was an untidy pile of splinters stretched along the broken banks, with bloated bodies of cattle intermingled. Others were caught in eddies and small pockets of still water, legs standing straight up in the air. Maybe three or four, possibly five, roamed the brush in the foothills behind the crossing. They were all that was left.

He had to face facts: the herd was gone. Which meant Zachariah Clay had no funds now to sink into the proving-up of his land.

'No point in me busting a gut trying to meet the deadline now. I'm broke. Fellers, I'll see you haven't made this drive for nothing.'

The three hired hands moved uncomfortably in their saddles. How could Zack pay them anything?

'I'll find work somewhere and I'll pay you something for the time you've put in. Won't be anywhere near what I promised, but it'll be something to see you through.'

Chess looked at the others. Frank was puzzled and shrugged. Dodds turned away, as usual not knowing what to say or do.

'Look, Zack, what happened couldn't be helped,' Chess started, but paused when Zack lifted a hand.

'It did happen. Bad luck all round. But you boys don't have to suffer for it. I'll find some way of squaring away for all your help. May take time, but I'll do it.'

And they had to leave it at that because he spurred away, looking for a safe place to cross the thundering river, back towards the trail to the home valley.

★ ★ ★

Burt Helidon wasn't a particularly big man: medium all round, except in his bank account which he boasted was the biggest in this part of the Territory — and he aimed to make it grow bigger and fatter.

He wasn't exactly a bully, just 'bossy', and there wasn't a more stubborn man in the valley; Burt wanted something, he kept worrying away at it until he got it. If he had to, he'd *buy* it, but he didn't throw his money around.

His main rival was Curt 'Dutchy' Haas, owner of the Windmill spread, which backed on to Helidon's Broken Bar H.

Zachariah Clay's quarter-section was just north of both large spreads, and commanded the river bend. Not that it was anything special, though it was one of the most picturesque sections in the valley, but the bend curved into the Saddleback Ranges, between two steep-sided but low hills.

A blind man could see it was an ideal place to build a dam.

Not that any spread in the valley needed extra water right now, but the summers were cruel at times and easy access to sweet water would be a big advantage.

Burt Helidon saw this and, though he

had no intention of building a dam in the near future, he wanted that section just to make good and sure the Dutchman didn't get in first. Burt didn't trust Haas: the man was likely to throw up a dam for the simple purpose of cutting off Broken Bar H's supply in one of the oven-baked summers, or at least dropping it to a trickle, barely enough for herd survival.

Of course, Burt Helidon could — and likely would — do the same to Dutch Haas if he controlled that river bend.

It was something that had been overlooked in the geological survey. When it was discovered that a section had been left out some lazy clerk had simply marked it as available for settlement six hellish months, sweating your guts out and breaking your back — or even a leg — and it could be all yours, even if you were no longer fit to work it as a small-time ranch or farm or whatever by that time.

But that was the way this country

had been settled.

Both Helidon and Haas had tried to get it re-zoned, each spreading a little money in what they figured were the right places. But they passed over some cash-strapped clerk and just as they figured one of them had to be successful, this clerk, peeved, had given the quarter-section to Clay to prove up. Zack saw immediately the potential of the land: not that he would ever have the money nor the inclination to build a dam, but he knew the potential would add hundreds, if not thousands of dollars to the value of his property eventually.

Now here he was, no more herd, which he had sweated blood gathering, no money to buy needed timber to complete the cabin dwelling that had to be part of the deal — hardly any money for food.

But that last was no real problem: he just had to take time to hunt his food. There were deer in the hills, prong-horned antelope, goats — cougars, too, of course — and fish in the creek. He wouldn't starve. But he needed cash; time was running out and Helidon had made one more offer — again, generous: he would send men to help Zack complete the prove-up but with the proviso that Zack sell to him after the land was given to him in freehold title.

Zack refused.

'I might not make it to the railhead on time, Mr Helidon, but I have to try.'

Helidon's eyes narrowed under their bushy brows that showed streaks of grey. 'You're being plain damn stubborn, Zack! I don't like that in a man.'

'Except yourself.'

The rancher's rather coarse features hardened. 'Exactly! Now, I've made you a fair offer. You think about it. I could just wait you out, or perhaps, make damn sure you didn't reach the railhead on time. Then I'd put one of *my* men in here on prove-up and when he made it, he'd sell to me.' He smiled thinly, heavy brown moustache twitching. 'So, I'll get it one way or another.'

'I can see that, Mr Helidon. And if I don't prove up in time, you can have it. I won't care then.'

Helidon frowned. 'Jesus Christ, man! What's wrong with you, talking like that? You don't care about it; take my offer!'

'I said I wouldn't care if I don't prove up.'

'Well, you won't, that's for sure!'

'Until I know — *for sure* — I care.'

Helidon compressed his lips, shaking his head. He started to leave the partly completed cabin, a three-log-high wall on two-and-a-half sides of the slightly raised foundation, paused, and said coldly,

'You're not the kind of man I want in this valley, Clay.'

'It's not your valley, Mr Helidon.'

'Not yet.'

2

Living

He was just thinking he would wipe the blood off his hands and forearms before it started to dry and get sticky when he saw the cougar.

He didn't actually see the animal, just a shifting of shadow back there in the deep evening shade in the brush. No sound. No warning of any description. Just a fleeting brightness of yellow eyes swivelling in his direction.

Zack's heart beat faster and he dropped a bloodstained hand to his hip, swore silently as he swivelled his own gaze to where he had left his gunbelt hanging from a stub of branch on a dying tree — a good three yards away.

It wasn't the first time the cougar had visited his camp: the second deer he had shot since returning to the section and hung for dressing had gained its attention.

He recalled how his heart had hammered twice as hard then as it was hammering now. The animal had growled, obviously more interested in the deer meat than the man. He had been wearing his gun at that time and he had stepped slowly away from the dangling, gutted carcass, his hand resting on the Colt's butt. No man in his right mind wanted to be this close to a hunting cougar, he could easily put a bullet into the animal if it leapt — and it *would!* — but the cougar would keep on coming and it would tear him to bloody shreds in its death throes.

He had backed away, inch by inch, palm sweaty against the gun butt as he brought it up slowly, thumbing back the hammer. Belly to ground, the cougar slunk towards him, but it must have been mighty hungry because its yellow gaze kept sliding towards the deer — and the pile of entrails and organs that Zack had removed from the body cavity.

As it crouched, muscles rippling, he glimpsed the pendulous dugs, the swollen, distended teats, and he knew this animal had whelped recently and was hunting food, not only for herself, but also for her cubs; if she ate well they would feed well.

All at once, he felt a kind of relief; why, he didn't know. The danger hadn't lessened any, but maybe he could do something about that.

Slowly he backed to where he had put the guts that he had removed from the deer on to a square of canvas. He held his gun in his left hand now, speaking quietly to the big cat: 'Easy there. Just — take — it — easy ... Here! See? Yours. Help yourself!'

He had stopped by the tarp, where he drew a deep breath and holstered the Colt, having to force his fingers to uncurl from around the butt. He stooped, picked up the slippery liver, juggled it — and froze briefly when the cougar growled and looked as if she would hurl herself at him. Hurriedly he tossed the organ and it splatted down a foot in front of the snarling jaws. The big cat jumped back with nervous tension and wire-taut muscles, crouched, ready to kill him — but then it must have smelled the liver, now close up, stretched its neck, its yellow eyes seeking Zack and holding to him as the long, coarse tongue darted out and tasted the wet, purplish meat.

It was obvious that it was acceptable to the cat: the tongue licked its lips, darted out again. Slowly the muscles unknotted a little as it crouched and bellied closer to the liver. The first bite was gulped down and, watching the still-frozen Zack all the time, the cat began to eat.

He backed away and reached his saddle and warbag lying beside his blankets on the ground. He felt better with the Winchester in hand: it was more powerful than a handgun and would knock a leaping cougar off its trajectory if it decided to kill him anyway.

But afterwards he figured he must

have died a dozen times over when the cat looked at him, or growled, or shifted its body weight. Still, it ate the liver, devoured some entrails, then all of the entrails. While he stood there sweating, wondering whether his legs would hold him much longer, the cougar stood up and its head moved from side to side as it made a sound like a growl and a cough combined. It took a tentative step towards him, paused, looked at the dangling, gutted carcass, the hide only half-flayed.

'No you don't!' Zack said, taking a step forward and bringing up the rifle. 'You've had your grub! And welcome to it. I'd only have to bury that offal anyway. Now *git*!' He waved the gun and the animal jumped back a few feet, an instinctive movement, the muscles bunching instantly, eyes slitting. 'Go on! Get outta here!'

He couldn't believe it! The cat turned with a throaty growl and, tail standing stiffly, trotted back up the slope.

Now it was back! This made the

fourth time it had come for more easy grub. He dragged the piece of tarp holding the deer's internal organs closer to the cat.

It was wary, but not as nervous or tense as the first few times, and he stepped back, closer to the tree where his gun rig hung, one hand reaching for the Colt.

The cat almost ignored him; not quite. It wasn't that trusting on such a short acquaintance, but it was definitely less threatening as it bellied up to the tarp and began to eat.

Zack smiled crookedly. 'Bet you got a fine-looking set of cubs, the diet you're on! Well, I'll be hunting a few more deer yet, trying to make a living of sorts, and you're welcome — I think that's the word! — to have the offal.'

He jumped a foot in the air as a rifle crashed and the cougar screamed, shot straight up, at least three feet, as if catapulted from below. Then it came down heavily, snarling, sliding down the slope towards him, fresh blood spurting from one shoulder, fangs and claws bared.

Zack swung up into the tree as the animal turned to snap at its own wound, then it bounded off into the scrub — not really 'bounded': the wound had thrown out its graceful motion, making it lopsided, staggering, but survival instincts drove it away from the point of danger, adrenalin covering the immediate pain.

It disappeared into the dark shadows, then Zack heard a horse. He spun with the Colt in hand, cocked and ready.

Two riders came out of the shadows, one with the butt of a smoking rifle resting on his thigh. 'I nail that cat?'

'You wounded him.'

'Good. Hope the son of a bitch dies in agony.'

Zachariah Clay, still holding his six-gun looked closely at the man. He had never seen him before but there was enough light to show the Windmill brand on the horse he sat, and on the mount of his pard. 'You work for the Dutch-man?'

The one with the rifle ignored the

question, looking around, making sure the cat had gone. 'Reckon he'll be back?'

'No. *She*'ll go and hide, lick her wound. Stay put a while, then try to make it back to wherever she's left her cubs.'

'Yeah?' The shooter showed a little interest. 'Might track her then. Kill them little bastards before they can grow up and start killin'.'

'You ought to track her and put her out of her misery.' Zack's tone was flat, accusing, and he saw the man frown. He was a lean rider, with a long, craggy face, not deeply tanned like a range man. His pard had a little more weight and a more rounded face, but his eyes were as bleak as the other's, his skin that same semi-pale shade: here were men who spent a good deal of time indoors, or in towns, anyway.

'I ain't wastin' time lookin'. I wounded it an' it'll likely die. If it don't, it'll be crippled some and mebbe a bear or a bigger cat'll tear its goddamn heart out. Long as it don't come back, she can go and die soon as she likes — or take a lo-o-o-ong time. That'd be better.'

Zack's face was sober, hard-eyed. 'I see you're an animal lover. The thing to do, friend, is go and finish any animal you don't kill outright. What's the sense in letting 'em die in pain? And this one with cubs not yet weaned.'

'You seem to know a lot about big cats.'

'Not just cats I'm talking about — any animal you wound ought to be put out of its misery. Your responsibility.'

The shooter smiled crookedly, looked at his pard, jerked his head towards Zack. 'We got us a real gen-u-ine cat-lover here, Lex.'

'Mebbe we better see we put him outta his misery nice an' quick, huh? After we gut-shoot him.'

Zack merely lifted his cocked Colt and they both stiffened. The one with the rifle started to move it but Zack merely shook his head — just once. Warningly.

'Do b'lieve he's feelin' froggy, Monte,' said the round-faced man, eyes narrowed to slits now, but he made no move towards his own six-gun.

'His bad luck,' answered Monte without taking his eyes off Zack, but also not moving the rifle from his thighs. 'Dutchy said you usually backed off trouble.'

'I can live without it. Had enough to last me a coupla lifetimes.'

Monte grinned, gave a short laugh. 'Hey, I kinda like this one, Lex. Well, cat-sticker, we just got a message for you this time. We know how you lost your herd an' you been huntin' deer, selling the venison in town and local spreads, doin' odd jobs — '

'Had to do something to make a living.'

Monte snorted. 'Call that *livin'*?' He spat. 'Dutch says you oughta know by now you ain't got a hope in hell of provin' up, so why don't you get out so he can put in a claim for your land?'

'Him and Burt Helidon.'

'Aw, yeah, he knows about Helidon, but he don't bother Dutch none. Don't think he really wants your lousy bit of land, just aims to make sure Broken H don't get it. That way, he won't have to worry about Helidon throwin' up a dam some time and controllin' the waterflow downstream — where Windmill is.'

'My time's not up here yet: I aim to work it out to the last minute. Tell the Dutchman that.'

'You wrong, feller,' Monte said with a grin that held no trace of humour. 'Your time is up here. But Dutchy ain't a hard man. He says he'll give you till the end of the week — give you time to sell off your tools and spare broncs, 'cause you sure as hell won't be needin' 'em.'

Zack flicked his brown eyes from one man to the other. They were tough and they were confident. Their gun rigs showed little signs that they were professionals: a cutaway on the outside holster lip to allow the finger to reach

24

the trigger a shade faster; Lex's holster was cut way down, leaving almost half his gun exposed, but just enough to hold it below the point of balance, so he could get it out more quickly.

Monte had contented himself with the cutaway for easier access to the trigger, and, looking more closely, it seemed to Zack that the front of the trigger guard itself had been cut off, opened, making an easy sweep for the finger straight to the trigger itself, instead of probing in from the side.

This man figured to have that trigger depressed and hammer cocked before most of the pistol had cleared leather.

Gunfighters — hired by Curt Haas. Things didn't look so good for the valley, with wild guns like this moving in . . . *Monte* — ?

'You'd be Monte Harte?'

The lean man smiled, genuinely pleased at the recognition. 'That's me, *amigo*. Don't get scared: I ain't gonna kill you — today.'

Zack smiled faintly. 'I'm not scared.'

Monte's face straightened and Lex frowned.

'Well, you damn well oughta be! You know Monte's rep?'

Zack nodded. 'Well, I know he don't like animals. Guess he don't care much for men, neither. A killer, I heard, notches his gun butt, but I don't see anything on that Colt he's wearing.'

'That's just talk.' Monte tapped his temple. 'I keep score up here. Nineteen as of last week. Down in El Paso . . . '

'Hadn't heard about that one,' Zack admitted. 'Last count I heard was thirteen. I wondered if that was gonna be an unlucky number for you.'

Monte Harte guffawed. 'No number's unlucky for me, feller! For the fool who tries his speed agin me, yeah, but not me.'

'We all have a number that's gonna come up sometime, Monte,' Zack told him and Harte laughed louder, more derisively.

'You b'lieve that, you'll b'lieve anythin'.'

'Yeah. I am kinda naïve, I guess. Well, if you fellers have finished delivering your message I've got work to do. Have to finish dressing out this deer for one thing — '

Lex Bates swore. 'Hear that, Monte? Son of a bitch is tellin' us to vamoose because he has work to do.' He leaned forward in the saddle. 'You dumb bastard. We just been tellin' you you don't have no work to do here, an' won't ever again! Pack up and git — or we'll make you.'

Monte held up a hand. 'Be fair, Lex. Dutch said put the clock on him — give him a week. And that's all you got, Clay. One week. You're still here after that, you'll be here for ever — six feet under the sod.' He smiled crookedly and touched a hand to his hat brim. 'Think about that.'

Zack said nothing, and Lex said,

'Oh, by the way, almost forgot. Me an' Monte, we ain't real cowboys, you know, not all that experienced with ropin' an' ridin' and all that frontier stuff. So we have to say sorry — some of Dutchy's cows got away from us and wrecked that south fence of yours. Knocked it flat, almost buried in the mud by the crick. Be a helluva job diggin' it out an' rebuildin.'

Zack stiffened, frowning. 'When was this?'

Lex's grin widened and he glanced at Monte as both men lifted their reins.

'When was it, Monte?'

Harte glanced over his shoulder at Zack. 'Tomorrow mornin', I believe — just before noon!'

Both men laughed and dug in the spurs.

Zack watched them ride away, then returned to the job of dressing out the deer. Afterwards he walked down to the creek and washed up, pulled on his old shirt and whistled up his buckskin.

After wrapping the cuts of meat in burlap and stowing the packages high in the tree, covering them with a wet tarp, he rode out. When clear of his campsite, he began following the staggering tracks of the wounded cougar, seeing splotches of blood standing out scarlet against the ground.

With luck he would catch up with it before the light faded completely.

He would have to do the humane thing and kill it with a quick bullet; the cat would be no good with a shattered shoulder. He couldn't help wondering where the cubs were hidden, and whether they were big enough yet to look after themselves if the mother never returned.

Maybe he ought to forget about the big cat and its cubs and go shoot Monte and Lex.

That would likely make more sense.

It was what he should have done.

3

Dying

Three days later, after tracking the wounded cougar and putting it out of its misery — he could not find the den with the cubs — Zack was again in the main street of Benbow, the only town in the valley. Strictly speaking the settlement wasn't in the valley, but a couple of miles outside it.

Zack Clay had more venison with him and the dressed and ready-for-tanning deer hides. He could get himself a few extra dollars for those: the meat was already sold, pre-ordered. Folk liked fresh venison, especially the way Zack did his: he always hung the dressed deer overnight before dissecting it into the various cuts — pot roasts, cutlets, steaks and so on, those extra hours allowing the juices to gather, tenderizing the meat as well as giving it full flavour.

With the few dollars he had made doing odd jobs for ranches and townsfolk, he felt able to pay Chess, Frank and Dodds at least some of what he owed them, or what he figured he owed them: *they* were quite happy to write off the experience, although none of them could reasonably afford the loss. But they were good men, knew no blame could be laid upon Zack, not even the relentless pursuit of the murderers of the ferryman's family; as he had said, someone had to avenge them.

That was still something of a mystery to all three, and to others they had mentioned it to upon their return to Benbow. Everyone taken into their confidence was puzzled — Zachariah Clay had been known as a quiet, unassuming man since his arrival in the valley. He had made it clear enough he wouldn't be wronged or insulted, but also made it obvious that he didn't look for trouble.

There hadn't been any to speak of; certainly no one had ever suspected the ruthless side he had shown at the ferry landing on the trail to Two Peaks.

Naturally, there were some folk who figured he was short on grit, when he would rather settle arguments with a few succinct, well-chosen words that didn't give offence.

These folk were wrong but wouldn't be convinced.

But, this day, before Zack rode back to his campsite on his quarter-section at Bowleg Creek in the valley, the whole damn town would see just what kind of man Zack Clay really was.

There was no law as such in Benbow. No sheriff or permanent deputy; sometimes a couple were hired when a trail herd was passing through. This was happening more and more frequently as the trail men pioneered a new route to the expanded saleyards at Two Peaks, just to keep the wild crews in some sort of order.

Benbow wasn't a town that needed

the kind of fulltime law that a gun-hung sheriff could provide. Folk got along together, in the main, pretty darn well. Sure, there was the occasional brawl, mostly on a Saturday night when the boys in from the valley hit the lone saloon for a few drinks and sometimes a temper or two slipped a cog and fists flew.

Bygones were bygones after a couple of bracing drinks. Sometimes these were on the house if the saloon man, Kelly Trevise, felt the fight had provided some good entertainment.

But the Dutchman had never cared for Zack, regarded him as spineless, and passed this information along to his two new hardcases, Lex Bates and Monte Harte.

So they were mighty confident when Zack came out of the saloon after insisting that Frank and Dodds take the few dollars he offered. Chess had taken a job riding with a trail herd: his money would be waiting for him upon his return.

Zack didn't notice the hardcases as he counted the few coins remaining for himself, trying to figure what to spend them on: coffee, salt, flour, or a log-splitter. There was a new tool on the market that was really a combination hammerhead and wedge on a long hickory handle. A man needed a sharp and straight eye to use it, but it made cutting planks a one-man operation instead of two.

'You fix that fence yet? The one our cows trampled? Accidental, o' course!'

Zack looked up slowly, saw Lex and Monte standing at the edge of the walk. It had been Monte who had spoken. 'Not yet.' He went to step around them but they blocked his way and he stared silently for a moment, pocketed the coins, set down a small parcel containing a worn shirt he had had repaired by the town's dressmaker. As he straightened to face the men they crowded him back against the clapboard wall.

People using the boardwalk, suddenly stopped, took in the situation at a glance, and then moved hurriedly around the trio, the womenfolk looking back over their shoulders apprehensively. A man having a quiet beer at the saloon batwings suddenly called back into the bar over his shoulder,

'Hey, fellers! Come looky here! Quick!'

He heard the lazy drinkers inside move their chairs back and stomp down the sawdusted floor to join him at the batwings, just in time to see Monte hit Zack's right shoulder with the heel of his left hand, spinning the man against the wall as he started forward.

'You huntin' trouble, Clay! Dutchy told you you had a week, but you been workin' on that damn cabin, in between time huntin' deer and butcherin'. You ain't made a single move yet to start packin' up or sellin' off your tools!'

'Seems to us you're thumbin' your nose at Dutchy — and Monte and me,' chipped in Lex.

Zack flicked his brown gaze from one man to the other. There would be no walking away from this, he decided, no calm words would deter these two. The Dutchman had obviously sent them in to give him a rousting where the whole town could see. Deliberately, he put a thumb under his nose and waggled his fingers. 'Told you I was staying.'

'And we told you to git!' Monte settled his boots and his nostrils flared as he sniffed, it was something Zack had heard Monte Harte did before he pushed a man into going for his gun.

Zack was wearing his Colt, of course, but he reckoned this could be settled without gunplay — and it had to be settled, there was no doubt about that, one way or another. Settled *now*.

'I told Burt Helidon a little while back that he doesn't own the valley. Now I'm telling you that the Dutchman don't own it, either.'

'Well, you see, that don't matter at all,' Monte Harte said, face grim and tight in its expectancy. 'We're telling *you* to pack up and get out. Who cares who owns the valley? You ain't wanted here, Clay; that's what it comes down to.'

'That's it,' Lex Bates said, coming in a little late as usual. 'Now you wanna ride out — or stay? But I gotta tell you, it'll be permanent if you decide to stay . . . ' He smiled crookedly at Harte and right on cue the gun-fighter said,

'Yeah. Change of address — care of Boot Hill.'

Zack was already shaking his head and he saw Monte's shoulders tense, knew the man was about to draw.

He took a quick, long stride forward, slamming his worn high-heeled riding-boot down on Harte's instep. The man yelped and danced madly on one leg, crashing against the wall. Zack kicked his other leg from under him so that he sprawled on the walk.

Before his face hit the gritty boards, Zack drove an elbow into Lex Bates's ribs and the man gagged, his hand falling away from the six-gun he had been reaching for, grabbing at his throbbing ribs. Zack followed through with a hammerblow to the chest, then clipped Lex on the jaw. He fell over Monte who was starting up, and both crashed in a tangle on the walk.

Men were running from all over Main to see what was happening. Zack knew he had to finish this now he had started it. He kicked Lex in the ribs — the man was uppermost, crushing Monte beneath him — and he yelled loudly as his ribs bent again with the impact. Zack knocked off his hat, twisted his fingers in the man's greasy black hair and slammed his head into the clapboards. As Bates sank back in a half-sitting position his eyes crossed and his jaw hung loosely, Zack turned to Monte, who had gotten his second wind and was bouncing to his feet now. He reached for his gun but Zack drove a punch against his jaw, staggering him.

Monte blinked and, rage driving him now, lunged back with arms working like pistons. The sheer weight of his sudden attack drove Zack off the boardwalk and into the street. Harte came after him, arms still working, trying to make violent contact.

Zack suddenly stood his ground, took three hard body blows, then brought his own fists up, parried a punch at his head, ducking under the arm and coming up, his face only inches from Monte's as he rammed a short, bone-busting jab into the man's midriff. Sour breath exploded into Zack's face and he stepped back, grimacing. Monte staggered, his knees wobbling.

But he managed to stay upright, then fell against Zack, threw his arms around his upper body, pinning Zack's arms to his side.

'Lex! Lex!' Monte yelled, gasping.

Bates shook his head, wiped blood out of his eyes and came lunging back, swinging. Zack lifted his boots and Lex ran on to them, spun to one side. Zack continued the backward pressure and Monte stumbled. In a moment Zack was free, whirling, fists hammering Harte around the head and upper body. Monte couldn't keep his feet under him, went down on one knee . . . just in the right position for Zack to snap his own knee up into Monte's already bloody face.

The hardcase stretched out on the dirt of Main Street, arms flung wide; like some bedraggled crucifix he lay there bleeding and groaning.

Lex Bates, groggy, came in swinging wildly. Zack moved his head aside, slammed one of the man's arms out to the left and brought up his elbow under Bates's jaw. Teeth chipped and blood flowed from his mouth, then Bates was crammed back by hard knuckles smashing his lips against what was left of his front teeth.

His head snapped back and he stumbled quickly; his heel caught on the edge of the walk and he fell, an arm coming up over his face protectively. He was clearly dazed and as Zack stood over him, fists clenched down at his sides, breathing hard, someone in the crowd yelled,

'Zack! Watch out!'

He spun, right hand instinctively slapping his gun butt, and saw that Monte Harte had managed to get to his feet. His Colt was starting to leave the holster, Monte's finger was already on the trigger through the cutaway in the leather and the open guard; the hammer was going back.

People scattered off the boardwalk, leaving Zack exposed, alone, a fine target . . .

'Then how come,' someone asked afterwards, 'it was Zack's gun that blasted and two spurts of dust jumped from Monte's shirtfront and he was flung out into the middle of the street. Huh? How — the — hell — come? I mean, Harte's a known gunslinger, a killer, half-brother to a bolt of lightning, had his gun almost free, and cocked, yet Zack dropped him in his tracks!'

After shooting Monte, Zack spun swiftly, obviously some inbuilt instinct driving him in such a situation. His smoking gun came around to line up with Lex Bates who was lifting his Colt, snarling as he triggered.

Lex was just too blamed mad, allowed his rage to take over, so that he was trembling and shaking and couldn't have hit the side of the saloon if he'd turned to face it, although standing only six feet away.

Zack's Colt blasted a split hair after Bates's weapon. Lex slammed back into the clapboard wall, legs folding, the back of his head rapping every overlapping board until he sat down with a jolt, then slowly toppled on to his side.

Above the dying echoes of the gunshots someone said with a ton of feeling,

'Jesus wept!'

★   ★   ★

'It was a fluke,' Zack Clay maintained, looking around at the small, tight group of Benbow businessmen who had invited him into the back room of Magee's General Store, just as he was getting ready to leave town.

42

The dead gunslingers had been toted off to the happy undertaker: happy for the business, for there wasn't much of it in Benbow these days; a man would never get rich in this trade, in this valley, waiting for folk to die of natural causes.

The men had all congratulated Zack on shooting down the two hardcases who, apparently, had been making nuisances of themselves around town for days.

'You're the kind of man we need as town marshal,' insisted Judge Royce Granville. There were instant murmurings of agreement by the others in the big storeroom.

That was when Zachariah Clay insisted his gunning-down of Monte Harte and Lex Bates was no more than a 'fluke', adding, 'I'm damn lucky to be standing here telling you that right now.'

The judge, like all balding men with hair disappearing on top, had 'wings' of thick hair on the sides of his head, almost obscuring his ears. He brushed his palsied hands over this hair, flattening it briefly as he smiled.

'Zachariah, you are being too modest! No, no, don't deny it! Man, half the town witnessed that brawl — the fisticuffs were spectacular in their own right, I might add, and once Harte had decided to reach for his gun — well, your actions, or reactions, whatever you wish to call them, were almost unbelievably fast.'

Zack raked the group with a deliberately blank gaze.

'I'm no gunfighter. If I had to go up against someone like those two again, you'd likely have to bury me.'

Several voices disagreed — well, all disagreed, but some more loudly than others.

He let them go until the protests died down, then said, 'I don't have time to go through all the malarkey associated with an election, anyway, Judge, I have work to do on my quarter-section and the time limit's looming fast.'

'We can come to some arrangement

about that. And there will be no election.'

Zack's eyebrows lifted in twin arcs. 'Then your sheriff, whoever he is, won't be legal . . . '

The judge lifted one knotty, rheumatoid finger and shook it, smiling behind the movement. 'I'm retired, Zachariah, as you know. But I was a practising judge for more years than you've got on you and I know my law. You're right, though, a sheriff must be elected by the people of the county — but a town *marshal* can be appointed by a select committee.' He waved one arm about him at the men behind him in the room. 'This is select enough; we represent the townsfolk and we are offering you an appoinment as marshal of the town of Benbow, Bigelow Valley, in the County of Peony, Colorado Territory.' He glanced around at the businessmen. 'Shall we say a salary of one hundred dollars a month? And possibly a liberal bounty on every drunk you arrest and get off the street?'

A couple blanched but the majority nodded in agreement. Judge Granville smiled expansively. 'There you have it, Zack. You must admit it is a generous offer. All you have to do is keep law and order in the town when the trail herds arrive, which they will be doing any time now, on their way to the railhead at Two Peaks. The rest of the time you can work your spread. What do you say?'

Zack's first inclination was to merely shake his head and leave. He had started to do this but, catching the first signs of alarm on the faces of the group, he paused.

'I'll do it — for two hundred dollars a month, and forget the drunks' bounty.'

His words stunned them and there was a moment of silence when the whole world appeared to stand still. Then the protests and straight-out refusals began, everyone talking at once. Zack dabbed at a bleeding lip with a corner of a kerchief, poked a loosened tooth with the tip of his tongue, then took a tobacco sack and some papers from his torn shirt pocket and began to build a smoke. By the time he had it burning, they had calmed down and the judge cleared his throat.

'We didn't expect you to hold us to ransom this way, Zachariah! We know you as a decent man, a hard worker, staying out of trouble. However, I must say we were all somewhat surprised — and disturbed — to hear about your relentless manhunt and its — er — bloody conclusion at San Marcos Crossing. But in view of the heinous nature of the crime, I guess that can be explained.'

'That's over and done with, Judge,' Zack broke in curtly. 'Can you meet my offer or not?'

'I — don't care for your tone, young man!'

'I guess I'm impatient to get back to my land, Judge. The Dutchman has had his hardcases run cattle along my south fenceline and it needs repairs — and I need money to buy the necessary wire and posts. And Burt Helidon's not going to leave me alone for much longer, either.'

'After today, I wouldn't bet on that!' opined Magee, the store-owner. A couple of others nodded their agreement.

'No, Helidon'll be around. I saw some of his new 'ranch hands' crossing my creek yesterday. They looked like *compadres* of Harte and Bates. Which is why I want the two hundred dollars. I'll take my salary of a hundred a month, but I'll use the rest to pay Will Chess and mebbe Frank Marney to help get my land ready for the prove-up deadline, while I take care of the town. I can't do both jobs. And I want that land developed on time so that it's mine.'

'Give you a solid stake in the county,' the judge said, nodding sagely. 'Yes, I can understand that.'

Zack neither agreed with nor denied the supposition.

'I think you other men will agree?' The judge glanced around, got some nods as well as a few blank noncommital looks. 'With trail herds already on their way here, we have to make a decision. And I for one can't even imagine who we could find to do the marshal's job as well as I believe Zachariah Clay can. Come, gents! We have to make that decision right now.'

It took several minutes, a few men still holding back, but in the end, when Clay ground out his cigarette butt under his boot, hitched his gunbelt, set his hat, obviously preparing to leave, all the hands were lifted, making it a unanimous decision.

Judge Granville shook Zack's hand enthusiastically.

'Welcome to your new job, Marshal Clay!'

4

Raw Deal

Will Chess returned to Benbow two days later, after paying off from Hi-ho Handy's trail herd.

Like Frank Marney, Chess was a married man; his wife was pregnant and, because of low beef prices this early in the season after a prolonged drought that had almost turned the county into a dustbowl, her pregnancy would use up almost all of what he had earned.

So he was glad to accept Zack's offer to work the quarter-section along with Frank Marney. Dodds had been offered work, too, but was content to settle for the odd few dollars he brought in doing roustabout jobs, and drinking or gambling the money away at the first opportunity.

'Wish I'd been here to see that gunfight,' Chess told Zack. 'Whole blame town's talkin' about it. You been hidin' your light under a bushel, friend.'

Zack gave him a sober look. 'Why the hell can't I get anyone to believe me when I tell 'em it was a fluke? I'm no gunfighter, Will. I was damn lucky, that's all.'

Chess returned the sober stare. 'You gonna be countin' on 'luck' to see you through the marshal's job?' He shook his head. 'I don't think so. You're too cautious and smart for that.' When Zack remained silent, he said quietly, 'Heard some talk while I was ridin' with that trail herd.'

'Talk?'

'Yeah. 'Bout a feller name of Clay Enderby.' He waited, but Zack's face remained set in sombre lines, brown eyes narrowed some, mouth a thin, straight line. 'You know Hi-ho's from down Leadville way and the Sangre de Cristo Mountains?' Chess looked hard but there was no flicker in those hard eyes. He

51

sighed. 'Can talk the leg off a pot-belly stove and have it doin' a heel-an'-toe in nothin' flat, old Hi-ho.'

'Everyone know's Hi-ho loves to talk.' It was a flat statement, as if Zack knew some comment was required and that one seemed neutral enough to fit.

'Yeah. No one's too sure where this feller Enderby is from, but it's generally accepted he come up from down Texas way. Some say he's on the run, but no one knows from what. Anyways, he settled into a piece of free-for-the-takin' land the Government was offerin' just so as to get that part of the country settled. Enderby met this gal, Lucy Bigelow; he married her an' time went by and he proved up, and went off to buy himself some cattle. While he was away Lucy, pregnant, was raped and beat up pretty bad. Turned out to be by a feller called Joe-boy Hanrahan — know the name?'

'There was a big silver mine around the Sangres I recollect hearing of once.' Zack's voice was very steady. 'Believe it was owned by someone named Hanrahan.'

'That's the one — Joe-boy was his son. Kid made a run for it, and the old man sent two of his hardcases after him. For protection. This Enderby caught up with 'em, killed one guard, wounded t'other who'll never walk again, then beat up Joe-boy and dragged him back to Leadville at the end of a rope behind his hoss, for trial.'

'Might've heard something about that,' Zack admitted carefully.

'Hell, whole of that part of the state's still talkin' about it. Old man Hanrahan wanted Enderby tossed in jail but somehow public feelin' against the Hanrahans stopped that. But the old man got to the judge, who let Joe-boy off with a year in jail, minimum allowed by law, then fixed it so's he could apply for parole in six months. During which time Enderby's wife died in childbirth. Complications from the rape, accordin' to the local sawbones. Baby was stillborn, of course.'

The hard brown eyes were dark gun muzzles staring out of Zack's white face.

'And some folk still believe there's a God,' he said with quiet venom.

'When Joe-boy's parole was granted — surprisin' no one — Enderby was waitin' for him the day he was released. Hanrahan had arranged for four of his men to meet Joe-boy who insisted on ridin' into the nearest town to celebrate. Too bad for him. Clay Enderby showed up, gunwhipped two of the bodyguards, shot one and ran the fourth man off. Then Enderby made Joe-boy buckle on a gun rig from one of the dead guards and told him to draw or die where he stood. Enderby nailed him, of course, and everyone said it was a fair shakes: Joe-boy had a better chance than he'd given Enderby's wife. The law didn't see it that way, went after him, but he shot his way past two deputies and rode the sheriff down, didn't hurt him too bad. But there's a bounty on him down that way still, put up by Old Man Hanrahan.'

Chess stopped, watching Zack, who eventually spoke. 'This Enderby; sounds like a real curly wolf. What happened to him?'

Chess smiled thinly. 'Not sure. I *think* I've got a notion about that, but it's really none of my business. Funny thing was, old Hi-ho said, at the end of his long-winded tale, 'No one blames Enderby, 'cept Titus Hanrahan. Folk'll tell you Enderby done the right thing, 'cause Joe-boy had that town buffaloed, things he done an' got away with because of his old man. They won't never forget Enderby over in the Sangres: Clayton *Zachariah* Enderby.' Queer how that name's not much different from yours, huh? If you turn it around some, I mean.'

'If you wanted to play with it, I guess,' Zack allowed without much interest, but there was a hard edge to his words. 'Think if I'd known this Enderby, I might've sided him in what he did.'

'Yeah, but he don't sound like he

would need anyone siding him, what-ever he was doin'.'

'No. He was crossed-up by the law and Hanrahan and set things to rights in his own way. Had no choice.' Zack said quietly. 'It's how a man ought to operate when the law lets him down and there's nowhere else to turn, way I see it. How do you feel about that, Will?'

'Me? Hell, I'm with you — with Enderby, Zack. Bet he wouldn't bother with the law none if ever he run across another rape of some poor defenceless woman, like that one at the ferry crossin', say. He'd settle things his way, make damn sure the sons of bitches, paid for it — like they did.'

Zack's breath sighed out lengthily. He smiled thinly and punched Chess lightly on the shoulder. 'Man after my own heart, Will.' Then he made an abrupt change of subject. 'Word is the next trail herd's only a day's ride away. I'll show you what I want you and Frank to do around here, then I better head for town and pin on that brand-new marshal's star they bought me.'

'If I wasn't sure before, I am now: you'll make a damn good marshal, Zack — and I'm sure glad I won't be crossin' swords with you!'

'*Gracias, amigo*. I hear Helidon has sent for some fast guns, after the Dutchman bringing in Harte and Bates — and losing them. You get even a whiff of trouble, send Frank in to me right away. I don't have any legal jurisdiction out in the Valley, but I've got a right to defend my own land.'

'I'll do that, Zack,' Chess promised, and thought, *Just the kinda attitude that Clay Enderby would take . . .*

★   ★   ★

The Dutchman sat his shag-maned paint a few feet from the front steps of Burt Helidon's sprawling log-and-adobe ranch house, sitting four square on its riverstone foundations, looking as impregnable as a Spanish fort. Curt Haas knew

Helidon wasn't going to be polite and invite him in, was leaving him sitting there in the scorch of the high sun, the sweat glistening on his pale skin. In all the years he had been working cattle on the American frontier, the Dutchman had never been able to keep a tan; freckles and peeling, paperlike skin over reddened flesh was the best he could ever hope for.

Helidon's bad manners now made Haas mad when he glanced down and saw the backs of his blotched hands already starting to redden.

'What is it, Dutchy?' Burt Helidon demanded, a bent stem pipe in one big hand, smoke curling from the bowl. 'I'm about to have my lunch.'

Rubbing it in! the Dutchman thought, and suddenly decided he was damned if he would allow his irritation to show.

'Mine'll be waitin' for me back at Windmill,' he said in his gravelly voice, the accent making everything he said sound aggressive. 'Them men I lost to Zack Clay — Monte and Lex. Come

58

with good credentials, cost me plenty. Then that damn nester shows his true colours and guns 'em both.'

'You oughta be more careful who you hire. Don't believe everything you hear. Do some close checking. I do.'

Dutch Haas stiffened, frowning, his long, washboard face tightening. 'You — been hirin'?'

Helidon shrugged, took a puff or two on the pipe before answering. 'Why not? You can do it, nothin' to stop me doing the same thing.'

'Who you got?'

'You'll find out when they get here. But I'll tell you this much: Zack Clay won't find them so easy to smoke, like he did your pair.'

Dutchy almost smiled. 'He's wearin' a badge now.'

'Aaah, don't mean a thing. Hired gun, that's all he is. Granville and his cronies just want him to protect their businesses, they ain't too worried about the streets of Benbow long as their profits keep rollin' in and the trail men don't smash up their premises.'

'Mebbe. But Clay has authority in town and I don't like it. It works in there, Granville and his friends'll find some way to give him jurisdiction out here in the valley if they figure they have to.'

Helidon smiled. 'Don't bet on it, Dutch. I've got too much invested in this valley to let that happen. You have, too.'

Haas's frown deepened and, slow thinking, he nodded after a moment or two. 'We — help each other, eh?'

Helidon laughed. 'I wouldn't go so far as to say that! Mebbe we can lend each other a hand for some particular problem, but 'help' . . . ' He shook his head. 'Not the way you meant it.'

'Then you are a fool, Burt! A bigger one than I thought!' He tensed as he saw Helidon's big face tighten and the hand holding the pipe gripped it so hard that it snapped the stem. The rancher swore and hurled the now useless pipe over the porch rail.

'Watch your damn mouth! You're on Broken H land here.'

'I know! And I would give you the same kind of welcome if you came to Windmill. But it doesn't change anythin', Burt. This Zack Clay is dangerous, very dangerous, to both of us. You heard what he did to the killers of that ferry woman. And he was fast enough to kill men who were considered *very* fast guns! You don't realize just how big a problem the son of a bitch is. I came here to see if you wanted to join forces and get him off that quarter-section, once and for all, but if you want to go it alone, then you must realize you'll be against Clay — *and* me!'

He touched a hand to his weathered hat-brim and turned his paint, ready to spur away.

Suddenly, Helidon moved to the top of the short steps,

'Wait up, Dutchy! Umm . . . mebbe we ought to have a talk. Why don't you have some lunch with me and we can discuss things over food and a few good drinks. I've got some imported Scotch I been waiting for an excuse to open.'

Dutch was swinging down from his saddle, started to unstrap one saddle-bag flap.

'And I have some *imported* schnapps! We may have a pleasant afternoon, eh?'

'Mebbe. Let's hope it leads to Clay having an unpleasant time as town marshal. Come on up.'

As the Dutchman started on to the porch and Burt Helidon held the door open, both men had similar thoughts:

Each would use the other to oust Zachariah Clay from the quarter-section, but . . . *then* what would happen?

With the land vacant, which one of them would move in on it? And what would he do with it?

Before they reached the lunch table, both had reached the same conclusion.

The only way it could be settled would be by a range war.

5

Peace Officer

The trail boss was well known along the cattle trails, which had now opened a shorter route to Two Peaks by cutting through Bigelow Valley. His name was Blackjack Tom; no one in living memory had ever heard his last name.

And he wasn't about to tell; over the years several foolishly inquisitive trail hands and, once, a lawman down in El Paso had tried to prise it out of him. Most spoke with a lisp now, due to cracked or missing teeth, or as a result of a broken jaw that never healed properly. The lawman retired — early.

Blackjack was a short, lean man with a face like creased leather and a tongue like a bullwhip. He could cut a man down to size pronto with that tongue and, if it wasn't successful, then he had

63

large knotted fists out of all proportion to the size of his thin forearms, which usually finished the job. On a few occasions he had even resorted to the long-barrelled hogleg he wore cross-draw fashion in a cut-down Confederate States of America holster; the embossed letters 'C S A' within their black oval, picked out in red paint. He had a Montgomery, Alabama, accent that complemented the gun rig and the almost threadbare Confederate cap he wore atop his ragged thatch of greasy brown hair.

When word reached the trail herd, a few miles south of the valley, that there was now a no-nonsense town marshal in Benbow, he stared hard at the man who had brought what was meant to be a warning, then flicked his gaze to those of his trail crew who were within earshot.

'That scare y'all?' Blackjack asked mildly.

'Hell, yeah!' one man said, a half-caste Negro, putting a deliberate tremble in his voice, lifting hands from his saddle horn and making them shake exaggeratedly. 'I'se scared white, borss!'

That got a laugh and Blackjack's mouth lifted in one corner, as close as he ever got to smiling. 'Then they'll just have to serve you at the bar 'stead of making you stand outside the rear door and have it handed out to you.'

The laughter increased and a few other trail men added their derisive remarks.

'He anyone we've met before, boss?' a pale-haired ranny called Andy Gault asked.

Blackjack spat. 'He wouldn't be that big a fool. Once he knew it was our herd comin', why, he'd've resigned on the spot if he had any sense.'

A couple of men cheered; the trail boss had just set the mood for their behaviour once they hit town and got an advance against their pay. Zack Clay was a new challenge.

They could hardly wait to put the new marshal to the test.

* * *

The holding pens a mile out of town and on the valley side were barely visible because of the pall of dust eclipsing them. The atmosphere took on a golden hue as the sun set beyond the ranges, rays like a fanned handful of knives slashing at the gilt-and-pink clouds.

With the yells of the trail crew hazing the bawling steers in through the pole chutes and gateways it was a scene that might well have appealed to one of the artists who travelled the West looking for picture subjects that would entice city slickers out on the trail to Manifest Destiny.

Strangely, the constant cussing and violent movements of the manipulated horses — this way, *that* way, you blankety-blank jughead! Cut off that goddamn heifer! Shoulder that one-ear in to the chute. *Oh, Christ! Who cut out this walkin' bag of bones for me!* — none of this detracted from the overall picture as viewed from Main Street.

They had cleared a shed for Zack to use as an office; it had been a store for old fire-fighting gear before the new fire station, complete with horse-drawn pump-wagon, had been built. Magee had found an old scarred and varnish-peeling desk that would fit through the doorway, and Chancey, the saddler, had come up with two old chairs that had been thrown out on the trash heap — but he rescued them and fixed leather across the frames. They were far from comfortable but were OK for sitting in for short periods.

Zack's backside was aching from sitting on the one he had set behind the desk and, rubbing his numbing but-tocks, he walked out onto the small landing and looked across to the frantic activity out at the pens.

'Those boys're in a hurry to hit town,' he observed quietly to himself. 'Either they want the cheap beer Kelly's offering, or the painted women — or they want to see what the new marshal is made of.'

He favoured the last, and took out his six-shooter, checked that the cylinder carried a full load and that the hammer cocked smoothly. He rammed it back into the holster and drew it out again several times, testing ease of draw.

Some folk strolling by seemed to tense a little and even clutch each others' arms tightly as they saw him. He smiled briefly, touched two fingers to his hat-brim. ' 'Evenin', folks.'

One man detached himself from the two women he was with, obviously wife and daughter, and walked across. Zack recognized him as King, the local druggist. He nodded to the marshal and gestured to the six-gun.

'I — er — hope you aren't going to have to use that tonight, Marshal.'

'Me, too, Doug.'

'Well — er — do you need to — practise . . . here? Where womenfolk can be downright frightened just seeing you like this?'

Zack holstered the weapon, looked past the man and smiled at the women. 'Beautiful evening, ladies. Here's hoping we can keep it that way.' He lightly slapped the gunbutt; he didn't need to say any more.

Doug King tightened his lips and hurried back to take his wife's arm, dropped his other hand to the shoulder of the small girl. 'Let's get off the street, dear.'

By the time they had hurried along and turned in to the street where they had their home above Doug's drug store, the first of the trail men were wheeling and skidding into the far end of Main, raising dust, eager to raise hell.

There were seven of them. One looked like a half-breed of some kind, with swarthy skin and heavy features. Three drew their six-guns as they thundered into the main business block where the saloon was. A ragged volley of shots tore at the dreamy evening and the men shattered the peace further by cutting loose with war cries and Rebel yells.

One man noticed Zack and started to haul rein, first easing his horse to a canter, then slowing to a jog-trot, walking it towards Zack.

'Where's this here fire-eatin' peace officer we been hearin' about, feller?'

Zack shook his head. 'No one on that kinda diet around here.'

The flaxen-haired cowpoke frowned, fighting his frisky mount, looking hard at Zack. 'You wouldn' be him, would you?'

'I don't eat fire, friend. Occasionally I breathe it a little, though.' Zack flipped the left side of his cowhide vest open, revealing the shiny new marshal's star.

Andy Gault's jaw dropped a couple of inches, then he yelled at the rest of the crew, who were already dismounting with plenty of noise and high spirits in front of the saloon.

'Hey, fellers! I've found him! This here beanpole just showed me his badge!'

Gault dismounted and the crew

hustled down from outside the saloon, all staring at Zack Clay.

'You the one nailed Harte and Lex Bates?' asked a curly-haired man built like a beer barrel. Zack nodded and the man scoffed. 'I'd like to've seen that!' He turned and looked at his companions. 'I seen Monte Harte and Lex Bates in El Paso an' again in Wichita. I tell you, I never even seen 'em get their guns out. They was just there, in their hands, and the damn stupid lawman who'd braced 'em just died where he stood.' He flicked his gaze to Zack, who was still lounging against the wall. 'You distract Monte an' Lex somehow? Get 'em to look away and then drew an' nailed 'em?'

Zack shook his head slowly. 'It was a fluke.'

The men guffawed: they liked to believe that.

'Reckon it'd have to be,' said the half-Negro, who was called Hogue.

Zack merely nodded. 'Yeah. All I did was this.'

And the cocked gun was in his right hand, the barrel slowly sweeping in an arc that covered every one of the trail crew. The dismounted men seemed to be holding their breaths.

Zack looked down at his gun, as if puzzled, turned it this way and that — but the barrel was always pointed towards the cowmen.

'Never even tried. It just seemed to — jump into my hand. Like it belonged there. Queer, huh?'

The Colt was back in leather now but the men were finding it hard to relax, most of them looking at the gun rather than at the marshal. Then a shortish ranny spoke up:

'I'm Blackjack Tom. I've never heard of you, mister, but while you're mighty slick with that hogleg, I gotta tell you we is here to have us some *fun*! Our kinda fun. It can get a mite rough and — '

'I've trailed cattle, from point to drag. I savvy how you boys need to unwind.'

Looks were exchanged, with a lot of

puzzlement and slowly rising distrust; this wasn't the usual way for a tough lawman to talk: laying it on the line . . .

'Go have your drinks, just take it easy on the house booze. Kelly bottles lightning and thunder and labels it *Valley Whiskey*. Make sure you got a good pair of boots, 'cause it'll rot your socks and your boots, too. You know why the painted women are there. OK. Don't get rough with 'em. No slapping 'em around, they're only trying to make a dollar. Most of 'em have got their own hideaway guns, too, so you been warned.'

'Judas priest! What kinda town's this?'

Zack Clay sought the man who had spoken, a pimply-faced young ranny, face smeared with dirt and clothes heavy with a layer of grit; he was likely the drag rider.

'It can be a fun town, kid, you let it. You kick over the traces, and we're gonna tangle.' He pointed a thumb at the group, then at his own chest.

Someone later remembered that it was his left hand he'd used: the right was never far from the butt of the holstered Colt. 'It gets too bad, and I'll take your guns off you and lock you up. And don't reckon on joining up with your herd come morning. Judge Granville'll see you in his court and you won't just get a rap on the knuckles or a light fine. We're working up a chain gang here for a road we want leading to the east valley, and we need workers. So any of you fellers want a change from eating trail dust for a couple months, go right ahead and show me just what kinda hell-raisin' fools you are.'

Silence: all the trail men looking at Blackjack, who was studying the marshal closely with his hard little eyes.

'I think I seen you somewhere,' the trail boss said slowly, but got no reaction from Zack. 'Not quite the same name, but I was contractin' to the Hanrahan Mining Company a few years back an' — '

'Your boys're wasting time, trail

boss,' Zack cut in. 'Forgot to mention, everything closes down at midnight.'

'What! You got the clock on this dump?'

'Midnight. Better get started, boys. You want me, you'll find me here at my office.'

'What makes you think we'd *want* you!' growled Gault bitterly.

'If you get into trouble you can't handle, mebbe.'

They guffawed: best joke they'd heard this side of the Big Muddy! Trouble they couldn't handle?

'Man, that kinda trouble hasn't been invented yet!'

Zack nodded, touched a hand to his hat-brim and went back into the cramped office, which was lit by a smoking oil lamp, and closed the door. He heard their puzzled voices through the thin clapboard walls.

'What you make of that?'

'Either tough enough to back up what he said — or *din'* say — or he's plumb loco!'

75

'Ah! He's gotta be dumb, givin' us a pep talk like that an' expectin' us to take any notice of it . . . '

'Like no lawman I ever come up against.'

'Me, neither. Bet he's scared! Yeah, that's it! Scared an' tryin' not to show it.'

'The man's a joke!'

There was a short argument over that and it sounded like Blackjack Tom's voice that stopped everyone dead with:

'Way he got that Colt out was no joke.'

★   ★   ★

Zack ignored the first brawl.

Sitting in his dim office, smoking, half-dozing, even, he heard the crunch of breaking chairs, the tinkle of glass, the wild cheering of onlookers. *A fight*. He looked at the old battered cottage clock on the wall above the door. There was just enough light to read the time. Ten o'clock.

76

This was to be a test, see how fast he came running and how he handled things. The shouting was louder now but he ignored it. It would peter out of its own accord when he didn't come charging through the batwings.

He was right. The noise died away after a few more minutes and someone said clearly — must have been standing at the batwings for the marshal to hear the words so well:

'Reckon we ain't gonna see no badge-toter in here tonight.'

'How about them busted chairs and bottles? Who's gonna pay for them?' That was Kelly Trevise, the saloon man; he would be as keen as the trail men to see just how Zack was going to react to a little hell-raising. He wouldn't mind pushing it if it meant selling more booze and keeping the women working.

'We'll pay,' growled a voice that Zack thought belonged to Blackjack Tom. 'For this one.'

Zack smiled: if he hadn't already figured there would be a second brawl, likely a larger and more violent one, Blackjack had just given him notice of its happening.

It started just before twelve. Zack had been expecting it at about that time: see how he would break up the brawl — *if* he could — then watch how he handled the time limit which none of the trail men intended to observe.

A woman screamed; it might have been genuine, but he thought more likely it was an act. He waited. Sure enough, minutes later, someone started cussing out someone else. There was a roar of voices and then the unmistakable shouts of drunken men urging on the brawlers.

Zack stood and set his hat on square, loosened his Colt in the holster and went out. There was a sawn-off shotgun, made available by the town gunsmith, but he left it in the corner. They were waiting to see whether he came to the saloon armed to the teeth, or confident enough to just carry his six-gun.

That was how he appeared between the batwings, holding one side open with his left hand, using his right shoulder on the other — so that his right hand still hung close to his gun butt.

Half the crowd were watching the brawl; four or five men were wrecking the furniture and slugging drunkenly at one another, two painted women, holding their torn dresses over their bosoms but leaving enough exposed to keep the men interested, were cowering at the foot of the stairs leading to the joy rooms above.

The other half were watching the batwings for the marshal.

Someone yelled at the top of his voice above the din, 'Here he comes!'

All eyes swung towards the batwings; even the brawlers paused momentarily.

'Just hold it like that,' Zack said, starting into the saloon proper.

The fight started again by common assent; whatever had been the cause of it in the first place didn't matter now:

challenging the marshal to stop them was the main thing.

As the fists started slugging and blood flowed and skin peeled away under hard knuckles, the crowd began yelling, egging them on, all with half an eye on Zack.

'One more time: quit!'

No one took any notice of him.

'Get in there and do your dooty, *Marshal*!' bawled someone whose words were soon echoed by the eager crowd.

The marshal appeared not to take any notice of them. He walked forward at a normal pace, shouldering through the men who deliberately stood in his path, stomping on the instep of one stubborn trail man. He shoved the man roughly away as he hopped about on one leg and fell hard, howling curses.

Zack had to dodge a couple of wide-looping swings that 'accidentally' came whistling in his direction, then his gun was in his hand and the crowd scattered, some men shouting a warning.

Again, Zack ignored them, ducked

under a round-house right, came thrusting up between two of the brawlers and clipped the man who had swung at him on the side of the head with his gun barrel. Before the man had dropped to his knees, dazed and spitting blood, Zack rammed the gun muzzle into the midriff of the second brawler. He went down with a rush of beery breath, gagging and choking.

There were three men still standing, bloody and still spoiling for a fight — especially with the town marshal.

It wouldn't be fair to say they got it, because it wasn't a fight at all, really. Zack weaved and dodged and the smoky lamplight flashed off his gun as it swung, in short, forceful arcs. In seconds, the marshal was standing knee-deep in moaning, bleeding men sitting or crawling or sprawled on the scuffed, wet sawdust.

And the crowd was silent.

'Best order your last drinks, gents. This bar's closing in five minutes.'

'Hey! *Hey!* You wait up there, Clay!'

yelled the sweating Kelly, coming out from behind his bar. 'It ain't but eleven-forty — '

'Eleven forty-seven,' Zack cut in, indicating the old clock behind the bar. 'You're gonna lose a few minutes, Kelly. For allowing the brawl to get started.'

'Listen, you, don't get too damn big for your britches. Wha — what the hell you doin' now?'

Zack had grabbed two of the dazed and bloody men by their shirt collars, dragged them to the front of the bar and propped them in a sitting position. While they were holding their heads or dabbing blood from their wounds, he went back to the other three. He only had to drag one man across, two had staggered to their feet. He indicated that they should go to the bar under their own steam, then turned to Kelly.

'Give 'em each a beer and a shot. Charge it to your town committee.' He turned his back on the spluttering saloon man and looked at the scowling Blackjack Tom and Hogue the Negro.

'Get yourself a drink, black man — in front of the bar. And you serve him without bitching, Kelly. Rest of you men haven't placed your orders yet. I see by that clock you still got eight and a half minutes. But she closes right on the dot of midnight. Hurry it up, boys. I'll give you time to down your drinks.'

There was a rush to the bar and Zack found himself facing Blackjack, who looked up at him with slitted eyes.

'I *know* I seen you somewheres before. Makes no nevermind. You were as rough as you needed to be, just now, mister, no more. I can savvy that an' I thank you for it. OK. We see how things are gonna be. Tonight's the easy one, right? You showed what *could* happen if you really tried, but you were lenient, for which I also thank you. I still need to get some work outta these rannies and if you really busted their heads or locked 'em up . . . We-ell — *gracias*, you didn't.'

'Told you I'd done some trail-bossing.'

Blackjack shrugged and suddenly thrust out his big, gnarled right hand. 'How about I buy you a drink before you go?'

Zack smiled crookedly and gripped firmly.

Word would spread down the trails: *Blackjack Tom says the town marshal at Benbow is OK. Gives you room to unwind* . . . just don't push your luck.

Yeah. His job was going to be a lot easier than he had dared hope for, after this night.

6

That Damn Marshal!

Word soon went through the valley about how Zack Clay had handled Blackjack's trail crew.

Most folk reckoned he had done a good job; some were a mite leery: maybe he had been a shade *too* lenient? But only time would tell, and a couple, like the Dutchman and Burt Helidon, cussed; both men had been hoping that Blackjack and his crew would have taken care of Clay once and for all; then make Benbow a wide-open town.

'Damn that Blackjack!' growled Helidon, pacing back and forth across the large untidy ranch office. 'He must be getting old! Once he'd have dragged *any* town marshal down Main and dumped him in the nearest pile of hoss dung!'

What really annoyed Helidon was that he was annoyed. Normally, he could handle most things without raising his blood pressure, but that damn marshal seemed to have everything in his favour, just falling into place.

By now, he ought to be off his Circle Z, out of the valley completely. Helidon was poised to act as soon as this happened, aiming to make sure he would be first with the next prove-up application, which, of course, would be on behalf of one of his own men.

He'd already had a word with the land agent in town, slipped him a 'little something' to make sure the man's memory would be good and reliable when the Bowleg Creek Quarter-Section became once more available for another settlement.

When — not 'if'.

His man would be the Broken H *segundo*, Morrie Clegg, a good cattle-man, in line for the ramrod's job if ever the current man, Chris Fallon, quit

Broken H. Clegg was loyal enough, according to the pay, like most rannies. Put him in, give him all the help he needed to meet prove-up, then, after title was granted, buy the land from him — at a decent price.

No use skimping and giving Clegg cause to bitch and get riled, dig his heels in and hold him up for more money.

Just let him try! Just let anyone!

Helidon didn't trust that damn Dutchman though: if ever Haas got his hooks into what was now Circle Z, he could — and would — throw up a dam any time it suited. And then Broken H would be at his mercy.

'Not while yours truly is living and breathing!'

Helidon went to the side window. A group of men were repairing the leaking horse-trough down by the corrals and he picked out the checkered shirt favoured by Morrie Clegg.

'Morrie! Morrie! Get up here.'

Clegg, a big, lumbering man in sweaty,

dirt-smeared clothes and well-worn chaps, stopped at the office doorway, stomping his boots and scraping them on the coir mat there.

'Come in, come in,' Helidon said impatiently. 'Never mind the dirt. That crew able to handle the trough now?'

'Sure, boss. We'll have it finished by mid-afternoon.'

'You won't. You're riding into town. Couple fellers I've sent for will be arriving either on the stage or their broncs. Either way they'll arrive before sundown.'

Clegg frowned, mopping some sweat off his rather large face with its broken nose and scarred eyebrows. 'We don't need no more hands, Boss. I know round-up's just about on us but we got enough riders to cope, easy.'

'These men are coming to do a special job, not any ranch chores.'

Clegg was silent a moment, then nodded. 'They got names?'

'Tillerman and Ransome.'

Helidon watched his *segundo*'s face

register this news, the calm grey eyes narrowing, the stubbled, iron jaw tightening a little. '*Pistoleros*, both of 'em.'

'And all-round hard men. They're here to harass Clay, and I want 'em to start within minutes of arrival. Let him know they make their own laws; if they can make him look a damn fool in front of the citizens, all the better.' He walked across to the big iron safe with its chipped paint and big brass handle. 'Now, they'll want to see some hard cash, so I'll give you a couple hundred for each.'

Clegg whistled. 'This Clay's gettin' kind of expensive, ain't he, boss?'

'Not for much longer,' Helidon told him, almost smiling. 'Not with Tillerman and Ransome in town. He won't know what hit him — literally.'

★ ★ ★

First, Clegg checked at the livery: 'A couple of rannies asking for Broken H arrived yet?' No.

That meant they must be coming by the stage, due about mid-afternoon. He waited at the depot, smoking, passing time with a couple of punchers from the valley. Then they heard the rumble of the stage and the crack of Cockeyed Bob's bullwhip as he made his usual wild entry down Main, swung recklessly but expertly into Montana Street and brought the vehicle to a shuddering halt right smack at the hitch rail outside the offices of the Valley & Sierra Stageline.

Clegg drifted across and watched the first dusty and, it seemed, annoyed passenger step down. Others followed, looking none too happy. There was an obviously married couple, the woman angrily trying to adjust and set her hat on her black hair, clearly unsettled by Cockeyed's fancy arrival; a parson — that would raise some eyebrows: Benbow already had a padre and a local deacon; a muttering, soft-bellied drummer who had spilled something liquid that didn't smell like perfume down his vest; and a lone woman, auburn-haired, tall, willowy and beautifully clothed, with maybe a shade too much paint on her face: an addition to the saloon's bevy of fallen doves? No, a little too classy for that. But — that was all! *No more passengers.*

Frowning, Clegg stepped forward and grabbed Cockeyed Bob's thick right arm, the one he used to swing his bullwhip. Bob snapped his head around, the dusty fringe of whiskers fairly bristling. 'Let my arm go!'

Clegg needed no second telling: Bob's short temper was legendary. 'Cockeye, Mr Helidon's expectin' two — er — extra crew for round-up. S'posed to be on your stage.'

Cockeye squinted his good eye, lowered the lid over his wall eye, the one which gave him his nickname. 'Broken H hirin' gunslingers now?'

He sounded genuinely surprised but Clegg, glancing around quickly, shook his head. 'Nah! They're brothers. Like to put on an act, lookin' like gunfighters

the way they wear their Colts and so on
— actin' tough. You know: get a laugh.'

'Them two'd be about as funny as a
cholera epidemic.'

'Well, where are they?'

Bob shrugged, working at the harness
of the sweating, blowing team. 'Wherever Zack Clay took 'em, I guess.'

Clegg stiffened. 'What's Clay got to
do with it?'

'Met the stage comin' through the
pass, flagged me down, took off them
two 'brothers'. They din' look nor act
like brothers with a sense of humour to
me. Names on the passenger list are
Hank Tillerman and Carey Ransome
— and don't tell me they're not the
names of gunfighters. I've heard about
'em down in Texas and up in the
Dakotas, across on the West Coast and
as far east as Baton Rouge.'

Clegg nodded, frowning. 'How'd Clay
know they was aboard?'

'How the hell would I know? But he
took 'em off at gunpoint an' lucky they
was to have their mounts in tow behind

the stage, otherwise he'd've made 'em walk, I reckon.' He spat a copious stream, causing Clegg to step back quickly. 'An' them nags was mighty cantankerous, havin' had to swallow all that grit and dust kicked up by my team.'

'Where'd Clay take 'em?'

'Hell, I dunno, man. I was already behind sked. Last I seen he was headin' 'em south-west, through the pass, likely towards the Mesa Verde or mebbe the Ute Mountains. Now, lemme get unhitched. I'm mighty thirsty.'

Clegg stepped aside, still preoccupied. That Clay: never knew what he was going to do next. Clegg kind of liked Clay, tough, straight-from-the-shoulder, looked like a man who'd had it tough, but, well he was tangling with Broken H now and something had to be done. But what? He couldn't go on a wild-goose chase hoping to find the gunfighters, and Helidon wouldn't be pleased when he found out what Clay'd done.

And how the hell did Clay know about them, anyway?

* * *

It was simple: Zack Clay felt it was his duty to keep an eye on all new arrivals in town as long as he was marshal, so he telegraphed the stage depot in Creede and asked them to wire back a copy of the passenger lists on all stages coming to or through Benbow.

The names Tillerman and Ransome were easy to spot: he knew their reputations and the arrogance of their using their own names was no real surprise.

So he got his buckskin from the stables, stopped off at Magee's for extra ammunition, and headed out to Pagosa Pass, figuring it was the best place to stop the stage: narrow, studded with boulders, so not even Cockeyed Bob could make a run for it, should he be so inclined.

Bob was mighty riled, rounding the

bend at the southern end of Pagosa, to find a rider sitting in the middle of the trail, a rifle resting its butt on his thigh. He hauled rein and gritted curses, heard the thuds and small yells from the passengers as they were tumbled from their seats. He stood up, hefting the long bull-whip, just refrained from swinging it at the rider.

'*Goddamn*, Marshal! What the hell . . . ?'

'Hold the team, Bob.' Clay urged his horse forward as the door opened and the passengers, dishevelled and cranky, struggled out. Tillerman and Ransome came out with hands on gun butts, froze when the rifle swung down to cover them.

'You two stay put, rest of you folks climb back aboard. Now don't get excited, Bob. Just easing your load for you. You two, unhitch your mounts on the tailgate there — after you drop your gunbelts.'

Neither gunfighter cared for that and both looked quickly at the gawking, frightened passengers. Tillerman was the bigger of the two but still only about five feet ten. Ransome was a few inches shorter, had the harder face and the meaner eyes.

The one to watch . . .

'You got no authority out here, Marshal,' Tillerman said, running a thumbnail along his pencil-line moustache: a gesture intended to hold Zack's attention while Ransome . . .

'Move that hand a quarter-inch closer to your gunbutt and you're dead right there, Ransome.'

The gunman froze his minute movement, glimpsed Zack's deadpan face above the rifle and let his shoulders sag. 'We ain't done nothin'!' Ransome growled.

'And you ain't gonna, except shuck them gun belts.'

Purely for effect, Zack worked the rifle's lever and the cartridge already in the breech ejected through the open port, glittering briefly in the sunlight. As the lever closed, a new shell was rammed home, the hammer cocking with a solid 'click'. Nerve-jarring sounds to anyone on the wrong end of the gun . . .

Ransome was holding his breath now, wide shoulders stiff with tension. Tillerman let his own creeping hand fall loosely to his side. Two pairs of murderous eyes locked on the lawman. Then hands fumbled at belt buckles and the gun rigs tumbled around the gunfighters' feet. A jerk of the rifle barrel and they stepped away from them.

Watched by the silent passengers, who were far from relaxed, Zack had the men unship their rifles from the saddle scabbards and throw all the guns up on top of the stage.

'Hey, Marshal! I'm already behind schedule!' called Cockeyed Bob, dancing impatiently from one foot to the other.

'You'll be under way in a couple of minutes, Bob. These two aren't about to gimme any trouble. Right, boys?'

A murderous scowl was Zack's only answer from Ransome. Tillerman, touching his moustache again, said in a low, deadly voice,

'You're already in more trouble than you can shake a stick at, Clay. You're just too dumb to know it.' He snorted. 'But you'll find out soon enough.'

'Can hardly wait. Now let's get moving. On your way, Bob. Sorry for this, but has to be done.'

Just before he flicked the rumps of the rear team horses, Bob turned his one good eye towards the surly gun-fighters. 'Rather you than me.'

*   *   *

'Hey, where the hell we goin? It's gettin' dark!'

'At least an hour of light yet,' Zack told Tillerman, riding ten paces behind the two gunsligers as they made their way through Pagosa Pass, heading north-west now.

'You gonna turn us loose?' Ransome waited. 'We ain't got grub in our saddle-bags! Figured we'd be eatin' in town or out at Broken H — '

'Carey!' snapped Tillerman just too

late to stop his pard from mentioning Helidon's spread. 'Aw! Can't you ever keep your mouth from flappin'?'

Ransome glared at Tillerman, then at the marshal. 'So? We been hired by Helidon. What you gonna do about it?'

'Not sure. Could shoot you right now . . . ' Both men stiffened in their saddles, Tillerman instinctively dropping his right hand to where his gun usually rested, swearing when he realized it was no longer there. 'Save everyone a slew of trouble.'

'The hell kinda lawman are you!' snapped Ransome, not all that calm.

Tillerman curled a lip. 'He ain't no real lawman. Don't you recognize him? That's Clay Enderby.'

Ransome snapped his head around and squinted hard at Zack. 'What the — ? I thought I knew him. Yeah! It's Enderby, all right, little older, no mustache.' He grinned tightly, no warmth in it. 'They got a bounty on you down Texas way.'

'You mean this Enderby feller has . . . ?'

'Aw! Hear that, Hank? He's sayin' he ain't Enderby!'

'Name's Zachariah Clay.'

'And the stars are goin' out one by one,' Tillerman sneered. 'I seen you in San Antone, five years back. Nailed some Mex 'breed, called himself Ru-*dol*-fo Santos. Quick an' deadly — now one of the quick an' the dead!'

Zack said nothing but noticed Ransome watching him more closely, a deep frown carving grooves between those bullet eyes. Zack flicked the rifle barrel.

'Keep going. We're not there yet.'

'Where?'

'Keep going.' Zack jerked the rifle barrel again and, more reluctantly than previously, they continued walking their mounts deeper into the pass; it was darkening quickly in here with the rugged walls cutting out the slanted sunlight.

'Listen. I never heard you was a cold-blooded killer!'

'Not me, Hank.'

Ransome snapped his head around towards Tillerman. 'Wha — ? You think he's takin' us in here to shoot us?'

Tillerman kept twisting in the saddle, watching Zack constantly.

'Well?' demanded Ransome, sounding kind of tight now. 'Don't s'pose it's any use askin' you . . . '

Zack shook his head briefly. 'Keep riding. I'll tell you when you've reached the end of the trail.'

'Like — now!'

Zack was caught off-guard, Ransome holding his attention for a moment and, during that split second, Tillerman demonstrated why he was known as the one with the brains of this infamous duo.

He simply jerked his horse's head around with a violent yank on the reins. The mount, unprepared, whinnied and shook its head, but still followed the gunfighter's command, and almost jumped around, directly in front of Zack's mount.

Zack instinctively hauled rein, startling his horse again. It half-reared — and that was when Ransome did his bit. He

101

drove the spurs cruelly into his mount's flanks and it shrilled in pain, leapt forward, crashing into Zack's with the suddenness of a runaway train.

Horse and lawman went down in a thrashing tangle and his rifle fired as he squeezed the trigger involuntarily. The explosion was deafening between the narrow walls and the lead burned across the neck of Ransome's mount.

This happenstance was likely what saved Zack. The horse whinnied wildly as it rose, off balance, ramming against the rock wall, jamming Ransome's left leg. The gunfighter yelled an obscenity and tumbled out of the saddle, rolling and covering his head with crossed arms in an effort to avoid being kicked or stomped on.

Zack kicked free of the stirrups, jumping away from his crashing mount. He didn't land squarely but, staggering, managed to keep his feet for long enough to lever a fresh cartridge into the Winchester's breech.

Tillerman leapt his mount at him and

Zack jumped up on a boulder at the very base of the wall, pressing back, feeling the rocks grinding into his back.

He swung the rifle and the barrel sent Tillerman's hat flying, split the skin across his forehead. Face bloody, a firework bursting behind his eyes, he fell, was dragged a few feet and then sprawled in the dust. Semiconscious, he lay on his back, struggling to kick himself to safety.

Ransome was up and swinging a rock in one fist. Zack held his fire, dodged the blow, lifted a knee into the man's belly and slammed the gun butt on to the back of his head.

Ransome fell, face down, groaning.

When he came to, moments later, he found Zack's boot in the middle of his chest. He started to struggle up, found he couldn't move his right hand because the muzzle of Clay's Winchester was pressed into the palm, pinning it to the ground.

'*Don't!*' he screamed, his panicky voice echoing through the narrow cutting.

The terror in that sound brought Tillerman round fully and he blinked, straightened against the wall, holding his breath as he saw his pard's predicament.

Zack turned towards him. 'Seems to me the best way to get you gents out of the picture is to put a bullet through your gun hands. What you think?'

'No! For Chris'sake, no!' Ransome could hardly breathe in his fear.

Tillerman merely shook his head, seemed nervous of moving even that much.

Zack let them sweat it out for a long minute, then lowered the gun hammer, stepped back. 'All right. Mount up.'

There was no more talk then, just the slow, regular clop of the horses, echoing dully from the darkening walls.

Just as they cleared the pass Tillerman, holding a folded neckerchief to the gash on his forehead, growled over his shoulder, venomous, choking with barely restrained passion.

'Your'e a dead man ridin', Clay!'

7

Bit Moon

Burt Helidon jumped out of his chair, his legs knocking it over with a clatter. He had to lunge for the burning lamp on his desk and catch it as it toppled.

He burned his hand on the hot glass of the chimney and swore bitterly, settling the lamp, pressing the burned hand against his mouth and moistening it with his tongue.

'You mean — those — those *knotheads*, calling themselves gunfighters, let Clay buffalo them, *kidnap* 'em!' He jerked away from the desk, kicked the overturned chair, strode to the window and looked out at the yard, almost dark now in the dusk. He drove a fist against the windowframe and the glass cracked clear across like a thin, writhing worm. In disgust he bunched the curtain around his fist and punched out the entire window.

It was the first time for years that he could recall reacting so violently to bad news; this had really hit him where he lived. He wasn't a man totally without anger, but usually he could slap a lid on it before it blew, keep some control — but *this*! Hell, it wasn't just *bad*, it was downright *disastrous*.

He was breathing heavily when he faced the silent, deadpan Clegg, simmering down gradually. 'Cockeye Bob say where they went?'

'He didn't know. Just through the pass. Could've been headin' anywhere. Or Clay might've shot 'em.'

Helidon stiffened, frowning. Then he shook his head. 'No, Clay ain't that type. He'll make 'em clear the county, mebbe, or set 'em afoot . . . '

'Was a pretty smart move on Clay's part . . . ' Clegg cleared his throat when he saw Helidon's darkening face, and added, hurriedly, 'but he's got no real authority.'

Helidon snorted. 'He has — long as he's got a gun in his hand. Damnit to hell!'

'Them two, Tillerman and Ransome, dunno if they know the country, but they could find their way here just the same. From what I've heard, they ain't the kind to tuck their tails between their legs and run, just 'cause some badge-toter tells 'em to . . . even a hardcase like Clay.'

The rancher nodded slowly. 'You're right. By God, I've already spent good money to bring 'em here, paid their stage fares. I'm outta pocket if they don't show.'

'Like I said, they likely dunno the country, but we do.' At Helidon's quick frown, he added, 'I can take half-a-dozen of the boys and head out towards Pagosa Pass. There's a big moon tonight and if we shoot off our guns now and again — they'll find us if they're still in the area.'

'Good idea, Morrie! Get yourself some supper, an' pick your men — you've earned yourself a bonus.'

Young Gil Jeffries was the nighthawk on Windmill's south-west pasture, the one that angled down to the rocky rapids of a tributary of Bowleg Creek.

It was an easy chore on a night like this, balmy, with just a little breeze to keep things comfortably cool, big moon rising, spilling silver light across the countryside, a nightbird calling mournfully, the cows relaxed, silent.

He dozed in the saddle, allowing the trained mount to work its way around the resting herd; it would stop when it reached the starting point again, waiting for him to give it new commands with heels or reins.

Gil was humming some honkytonk tune to himself, half-asleep, drifting off towards full sleep, when the abrupt, alien sound of gunfire jerked him awake so violently he almost toppled from the saddle. The horse snorted as his weight shifted abruptly until he caught his balance again, right hand groping for the butt of his six-gun.

He shook his head sharply, trying to clear the last dregs of sleep, wondering whether he was dreaming. *No!* The echoes of the gunshots were still hanging in the air, fading, but definitely there. He yanked his Colt from leather as there were more shots, coming from the slopes of the sawtooth range that backed on to Windmill.

Way beyond, Pagosa Pass cut through another part of this same range, but the shots were much closer than that; thankfully, not close enough to spook the herd.

He suddenly realized, when the shots racketed out again, that they were in groups of three: the universal, attention-seeking volley used by someone in trouble, or maybe a search party, giving their quarry something to home in on.

After the fourth time, Gil took a long look at the herd under his control, decided they were resting well, not disturbed by that distant gunfire. He made his decision and put his mount down towards the creek and the shallow part of the rapids. He was young and not all that brave, but he had a strong sense of what he liked to call 'duty' and if someone was in trouble in these dark hills, then he was bound to lend a hand; it was his personal code.

The moon had cleared the range now and the light was stronger. Three more shots cracked through the night, moving away from him. He reined down on a small hogback, straining to see, thought he glimpsed a moving shadow that might be a grouped bunch of riders, two slopes over, heading for the crest of their range, taking them away from his position.

Search party, he decided, and he was making up his mind whether to go after them and see whether he could help when he saw another shadow — much smaller, much closer, in a field of boulders to his right.

A man, afoot and crouching, was making his way through the rocks, pausing to look after the party of riders — and not wanting to be seen, Gil figured.

He tightened his grip on his Colt, hoping this wasn't a fugitive and that those riders weren't a posse. After a moment, he called softly,

'What you doin' on Windmill land, feller?'

Too late he realized that the man had deliberately showed himself, so as to hold his attention while another man worked his way around behind Gil.

The first he knew of there being a second man was when a dead branch swung with a brief whistling sound and crashed across the back of his head, jarring his neck and shoulders. He fell out of the saddle with a grunt that was a combination of surprise and pain: dazed, but not quite knocked out.

Then, as he rolled, a boot pinned his wrist to the ground and his gun was quickly wrenched from his grasp. Gil tensed as he heard the hammer ratchet back to full cock.

'Hey! Wait up . . . ' he said breathlessly, slurring the words. 'I — I ain't — law . . . '

'C'mon down, Hank,' Carey Ransome called quietly to the shadow in amongst the boulders. 'I've got his gun — and we've got ourselves a hoss!'

★ ★ ★

The Dutchman was still awake — well, mostly so, sprawled in a big leather chair in his parlour. A couple of seams in the leather were split, allowing some of the stuffing to protrude. His legs in his stained whipcord work trousers stuck out, no boots on his feet, only dirty socks with holes worn in the toes by his horny nails. He was nursing a half-empty bottle of schnapps on his belly, his eyelids were getting heavier by the second, when he heard a horse come into the yard.

Frowning, he stirred a little, ran one hand over his thinning, fading hair and down over his leathery face, blinking. The crew had turned in long ago, so who . . . ?

'Who the hell's that?' he muttered,

stirring himself.

Boots thudded across the porch, the front door opened and he heard Gil Jeffries call,

'Mr Haas? Dutch ... ? It's Gil Jeffries. I got a couple fellers here I think you oughta see.'

'You think I oughta see, uh?' growled Curt Haas as he heaved upright in his chair, turning his head towards the office door. 'A damn cowhand, and *you* think I oughta see ... '

Young Gil was standing there uncertainly. His clothes were work-stained, his hair awry and he was holding a wadded kerchief to the back of his head. He came in, still unsure. Dutch saw vague movement behind the nighthawk and then two hard-looking rannies came in, one with the nighthawk's six-gun in his hand. Their clothes were torn in places, grass and leaves were clinging to them here and there.

They looked plumb tuckered out, but still dangerous, even if they weren't wearing gun rigs of their own, *and* there were signs of rough treatment.

'Now what the hell is this?'

Gil swallowed as the Dutchman glared, angry at being disturbed.

'These here are two fellers sent for by Burt Helidon, boss.' Gil was pleased to see that *that* got Haas's attention. 'Hank Tillerman and Carey Ransome. They was on the stage and Zack Clay took 'em off at gunpoint, up at Pagosa Pass, disarmed 'em and after makin' 'em ride through the pass, he set 'em afoot. Told 'em to clear the county and he'd shoot 'em on sight if they tried to come back.'

Dutch Haas squinted at the silent, sober newcomers, noting Tillerman's bruised and cut forehead, Ransome's gravel-scarred face and swollen jaw. He swigged from his bottle, wiped his mouth with the back of a hairy wrist.

'Heard of you fellers; you ain't here to work cattle. But what I hear don't go with what I see and what Gil just said. Can't b'lieve the men goin' by those names'd let no two-bit lawman take their guns an' run 'em off.'

'We're here, ain't we?' said Ransome. 'Windmill's still in Bigelow County, ain't it? So we ain't run off nowheres!'

Dutch half-smiled. 'A mite touchy there, eh? All right, s'pose you tell me just what happened — and what you're doin' here on my spread?'

Tillerman was spokesman now and told it succinctly, with an edge to his voice that grew harder as his story progressed. He almost choked up telling how Zack Clay had gun-whipped them both. A no-nonsense, brittle edge told Dutch the man was simmering inside; he would never forget his humiliation.

'Then when we got through the pass, Clay made us dismount, told us to get clear of the county, then rode off, taking our broncs. We couldn't do a goddamn thing. He'd already taken our guns and tossed 'em on to the stage. They must be somewhere in Benbow by now, I guess, unless that cross-eyed idiot driver tossed 'em off somewhere along the way.'

Dutch was still half-smiling, far from impressed. 'You boys don't seem to be livin' up to your reputations.'

'We was took by surprise,' Ransome snapped.

'Oh, I guessed that! Must've been all wore-out by that long stage ride with Cockeyed Bob to let Clay get the jump on you.'

'That's what you think, huh?' Ransome said grimly.

Gil saw this was going to end in some kind of blow-up as he watched Ransome's fingers on the six-gun restlessly tapping the blued metal.

'Er . . . Clay seems to be a lot tougher than anyone figured, boss. Hank here says he's a gun-for-hire, real name Clay Enderby, from Texas. Mebbe on the dodge.'

Dutch showed interest in that. 'Well, well. And Burt Helidon sent for you fellers, huh?'

'Din' tell us who we was going up against,' Ransome growled. 'Or we'd've asked for more money.'

Dutch looked quickly from one man

116

to the other. *Money, huh*? 'How much did Helidon offer you?'

He had to ask three times before Tillerman eventually gave him a figure, which might or might not have been the true one. But Dutch pursed his lips, nodding slowly.

'He's no skinflint, Burt Helidon, when he wants somethin'.' Haas paused, his thick lips moving once or twice as if he was calculating something. Then he looked squarely at Tillerman and Ransome. 'Fact, a damn good offer. So why'd you come here?'

'I — I guess I talked 'em into it, Dutch,' Gil said diffidently. 'Carey jumped me, took my gun and hoss. I told 'em they was a lot closer to Windmill than Helidon's Broken H and — and that you might be interested in — toppin' Helidon's offer.'

'Figured that out all by yourself, huh?'

Gil swallowed. 'I was — kinda scared, boss, after that clout on the head. It was all I could come up with.'

The Dutchman grunted, not looking

at Jeffries now, studying the two gun-fighters. Mean-lookin' bastards! Meaner than Monte Harte and Lex Bates . . . Hmmmmm.

'S'pose I was to offer you half as much again as what Helidon was payin' — to ride for me?' He waited; their faces were giving nothing away.

He needed someone to replace the fools he'd hired orginally. These two in front of him now had the rep, and he was willing to take a chance that they had been taken by surprise by Zack Clay, which was why they hadn't put up a better performance. They were mad as hell about it, too, which was all to the good — *his* good with a little luck.

'I'll supply guns and horses, ammo, anythin' else you need. Interested? You'd get a chance to square things with Zack Clay, or whoever the hell he is.'

The *pistoleros* looked at each other and, after a few seconds, smiled slowly.

★　★　★

Included in Zack's deal with the town committee, was a bed at the Regal rooming house on Bennett Street, where he could also have his meals but, before he could turn in, Judge Granville and Magee had come to his room for a brief, but uncomfortable session.

What it amounted to was that the judge was worried about how Zack had gotten rid of Tillerman and Ransome.

'You're a town marshal, Zack!' the judge said, irritably. 'You have no authority to stop a stagecoach and high-handedly remove two passengers!'

Weary after his long ride, and hungry, Zack was in no mood for Granville's hypercritical ways with what constituted his 'authority' and what didn't.

'You hired me to keep the peace in town, Judge. Letting those two in would've torn Benbow apart.'

'I understood they were hired by Burt Helidon, for work on his ranch,' offered Magee.

'You're not that naïve, Mr Magee.

Burt hired *gun-fighters*. There'd be no restrictions on where they figured *their* authority began or ended.'

Magee frowned thoughtfully. The judge was still acting prissy, serious but worried, too.

'You don't seem to understand, Zack. Statehood for Colorado is imminent. There'll be a county judge nominated and I make no secret of the fact that I want that position. Even though I'm officially retired, I'm eligible if I apply. My chances will be in jeopardy if you keep exceeding your authority like this. I mean, I'm on record as hiring you.'

Zack scowled. 'Judge. You know you hired me to keep toublemakers out of Benbow. Well, I'm doing that; just let me handle it my way. Ask around: you won't find many citizens upset because of the way I handled those *pistoleros*. Now I'm dog-tired and if you want the badge back, come see me in the morning. *Buenos noches*.'

Before the door closed, Magee nodded to Zack, mouthing silently: *'I'll talk with him. It'll be OK.'*

Zack didn't sleep well; over-tired probably, but he ate a large breakfast in the dining room, had three cups of coffee, then went back to his cramped office and rolled himself a cigarette.

He swung his feet up on to the desk, leaned back in his creaky chair and smoked slowly, eyes closed.

When he heard someone at the street door he opened his eyes quickly, swung his feet down and instinctively dropped his right hand to his holstered Colt, leaving his cigarette dangling from his lips. He squinted against the early morning sunlight, which briefly outlined the visitor.

It was a woman, and the sunlight, striking the newly painted door surface as she closed it, reflected on her.

He felt his heart stop, his jaw sag, as his hands almost splintered the arms of the chair, they tightened so convulsively.

'*L-Lucy . . . ?*' He gasped his dead wife's name before reason told him it could not be: she had been dead these past five years, but . . .

'No, Marshal. You're mistaken. My name is Penny Hatton.' Her voice was smooth, confident, and he made himself get control. *Just for a moment there, the reflected light showing her face, the colour of her hair, the way her jaw set slightly angled upward . . .*

His heart was hammering as she approached the desk; the way she walked, the set of her shoulders, wide for a woman — she was taller than Lucy had been, but, by God . . .

He cleared his throat, but his voice was still a little shaky as he gestured to the visitor's chair and said, 'I saw your name on the stage passenger list, Mrs Hatton.' He had noticed the wedding band on her left hand. 'Think I glimpsed you on the stage at Pagosa Pass, too. Sit you down and tell me what I can do for you.'

She sat easily, smiling slightly as she saw he was still staring intently at her.

'Forgive me, Marshal. I should've

said, I'm Penny Hatton, widow. My maiden name was Bigelow.' As he half-rose out of the chair, she added, 'I'm Lucy's cousin, and I've been searching for you for years.'

8

Lost and Found

They had been more like sisters than cousins, growing up as they had with their houses in the same town, though Lucy Bigelow's was one street over from where Penelope lived.

Their fathers were brothers, but Liam, Penny's parent, had fancy notions for his daughter that Lincoln Bigelow, Lucy's father, regarded as being way beyond achieving. Liam wanted Penny to be a businesswoman, an *active* businesswoman: a radical idea at that time. There were, of course, women in business then, but many were either financing their husbands' trades, or else they had become widows and inherited the business. Then they had a choice: learn for themselves or sell out — and likely be taken advantage of by ever-smiling, sweet-talking 'friends' of the late husband, who only wanted to 'help out'.

But Liam saw Penny as head of a string of drapery stores that handled expensive fabrics, imported from Mexico, England, and Europe, cutting out the middlemen, the whizz-bang fast-talking salesmen who always imported 'the best, not only in quality but in price — 'specially for you, friend!' She had a real talent for buying materials that appealed to rich women and sold well, was shrewd in her purchasing, marketing and even designing garments.

Liam had been burned early in his own career by snide dealers, had learned from his mistakes and over-confidence, so he knew his way around and set out to train Penny to take over as active manager of Bigelow's World Fabrics.

Lucy had decent schooling and opted for teaching; she was excellent with children of all ages and her father often jokingly predicted a large family for her when she eventually married. He never lived to see it; he had worked in the lumber trade, often taking up an axe just for the hell of it and the feel of his blood singing with the exercise of felling tall timber, as in his youth. He had been killed in mid-life.

A lopper, working high above him, cut too deep too soon and the top part of the tree folded down against the trunk like a closing book, tossing the lopper twenty yards over the treetops, and crushing Lincoln like a rat under the spring-loaded trapwire.

Link Bigelow had been well regarded and they named the valley where he had his stand of timber, Bigelow Valley, Benbow County, Colorado Territory.

Lucy's mother was dead and there were no siblings, so her uncle Liam took her in, much to Penny's delight.

They lived in Denver then, far from Benbow County, which Lucy loved. Restless, not comfortable with someone else providing for her, Lucy travelled all over the country, going from school to school, relieving vacationing teachers, replacing others where there was a vacancy. She made a little money and she was happy in her work. Her happiness was obvious in the letters she exchanged with Penny.

Then came the big surprise: Lucy was getting married. But she swore Penny to secrecy, not wanting Uncle Liam to know she was in love with a man who had a reputation as a gunfighter; he had been a lawman, too, but folk still regarded it as just the same as hiring out his gun. His name was Clay Enderby and she was exuberant over the prospect of the coming wedding.

The only faint shadow was that Lucy was being married in Tucson, so Penny would not be able to fulfil the childhood oath that she and Lucy had solemnly sworn: that each would be bridesmaid for the other when their wedding days arrived. Lucy wrote a long letter to Penny to explain. After the main contents there was a hurried PS in pencil: a true afterthought, it seemed:

Oh, Penny,

I have to tell you: I'm already married! It was a quiet wedding, and right after we had to leave for Texas — Clay was forced into a gunfight with some cocky young drunk, and won, of course — but the man turned out to be the youngest of a large, vengeful family of rich and powerful ranchers. They've been pursuing him — now 'us'! I will not be able to write to you again for some time — perhaps never! We're on the run. Oh, Penny! I'm devastated — yet I've never been happier, just being with Clay. Please try to understand. We will meet again, I promise.
Your loving 'sister',
Lucy Enderby.

Zack Clay was silent, easing his buttocks on the uncomfortable office chair. Opposite him, Penny Hatton seemed to be comfortable enough, after her explanations, though her mouth was drawn a little tighter and there was a brightness to her grey-green eyes that went well with her deep auburn hair.

Her hands, in white buckskin gloves with rows of small buttons on the closures, were in her lap, fingers intertwined. Her shoulders were straight, head held high and, with the brightness of sunlight now filling the small room, she caused Zack's heart to pound loudly to him — because the resemblance to Lucy was strong.

'Lucy told me she had a cousin named Penelope, but that she had lost touch with her and still missed her a lot.'

Penny nodded, taking a scented square of lace out of her left blouse sleeve, dabbing lightly at her eyes.

'Yes. She must have loved you very much.' At his frown, she added, 'To stay with you when you were on the run. I never knew what name she — you both — were using, though I tried to find Lucy, but apparently she no longer followed her career as a school teacher, either.'

Memories stirring wildly, he nodded,

his fingers tapping the desk top, his lips in a thin line. 'She made many sacrifices for me. We had to keep moving. Those damn ranchers were relentless. I heard one died a few years back, but I dunno whether the bounty they put on my head still applies or not.'

She looked at him soberly. 'And, of course, poor Lucy died, too. After my husband was killed in an accident — a train wreck in Mexico, while he was buying some newfangled sewing machine — I appointed a board of managers to handle my five stores and decided to start looking for you — to see if you could tell me about Lucy.' She said this soberly and he held her gaze until she looked away, but her tone was clipped: 'I still miss Lucy terribly! I've missed her for almost six years — since her marriage to you — when she virtually disappeared out of my life.'

'Guess she missed you badly, too. She was often sad, but always came up with a smile when I tried to find out what was bothering her. For what it's worth, I had no idea her marriage to me had caused any unhappiness — to you or anyone else. Not that it would've changed anything. But we were really happy together, tried to live within our own world.'

Those eyes — not as dark as Lucy's, yet the same shape, and stirring those memories again — studied him for a long, searching minute.

'You sound — sincere. And look it. I-I've never really questioned Lucy's choosing you; after all, it was none of my business . . . ' Penny paused as he nodded in curt agreement, then she heaved a sigh. 'I guess I was lonely, too — especially after I became a widow.' Her voice cracked a little as she added, with emphasis, 'Lucy and I were so *close*! I suppose I'm being selfish in one way, but — well, I'm not much more than a figurehead in my business now; other people run it for me, and very well, too. I decided to indulge myself, try to find you, and learn about Lucy's — last years.'

'I reckon I can savvy how you must've felt.'

'Can you? Perhaps. But I was fortunate in having money, so I could begin my search for you. I hired a Pinkerton man and he eventually discovered a clue which led me here. I arrived on yesterday's stage, saw you take off those two obvious gunmen. It was hardly the time or place to introduce myself. I thought you were very . . . tough, and wondered whether you were going to kill them. You certainly seemed capable of it.'

He chose to ignore the comment, in reality a query, one he had no intention of answering. 'And now you've found me, what next?'

'I don't really know. I wanted to see what kind of man you are and how you could've won Lucy's heart so totally. I never did know the full details of how she died.'

He had known she would get round to that and he did not want to answer, but there was no choice. He stood and went to the front window, looking out but not really seeing the dusty main street where horses drooped at the hitch rails in the hot sun, buckboards and wagons creaked along.

'She was attacked and raped. That should tell you enough, without my going into all the details.'

White-faced now, Penny sat up straight. 'Yes! Those — that news is shocking enough!'

'At the time she was pregnant with our first child. After I got back — '

'*Back*? From where. You surely didn't leave her after that ordeal?' She was outraged.

Ignoring her censure he said mildly, 'I tracked down the son of a bitch who did it and killed him. As I was saying, after I got back . . . ' It was his turn to sigh now. 'I guess the ordeal brought on the birth early. The child was stillborn and Lucy . . . didn't make it. Unavoidable complications as a result of the attack, they told me.'

There were tears on Penny's cheeks

now and she dabbed again with the lace handkerchief as he stared woodenly out of the dusty window. He started when he felt her hand lightly on his arm, smelled her perfume now that she was standing so close to him.

'You must have been . . . devastated. I suppose that's why you moved to this out of the way place . . . Bigelow Valley.'

She was tall enough for him not to have to look down much when he turned: her face was only a couple of inches below his. 'Lucy had often said she would like some kind of monument to her father here. After all, he did discover the valley. I was restless, rode in here one day and found there was government land for prove-up still available. I claimed a quarter-section out on Bowleg Creek where Lucy had often said her father made his first camp. I figured, if I could build a small place there, make a go of it — well, it would be a kind of monument to her and the memory of her father.' He sounded awkward, making the admission.

Penny's eyes softened even more and her gaze wandered over his hard-bitten face before she smiled slowly.

'My God! A gunfighter with a romantic streak! Or perhaps,' she said thoughtfully, 'perhaps it's an expression of true love. I'm beginning to see why Lucy was so happy, married to you.'

He turned away and looked out of the window again. 'I've run into trouble, though, with my plans. I may not be able to do what I wanted.'

He explained briefly about losing the herd he had counted on for giving him enough money to complete the prove-up conditions and how Helidon and Dutch Haas both wanted to claim his land.

'Maybe neither of 'em could afford to build a dam, but there'd be the threat of it and that would keep the one who didn't own the land toeing the line. Likely it would blow up into a range war eventually.'

'And you're working at being the town marshal. Will that earn you enough for you to be able to complete your land

135

requirements before the due date?'

'Mebbe not. I've got a couple of men working on it but Helidon and Haas're bringing in gunfighters. They're sure to start harassing us, so we may not make it in time.'

'What do I call you, by the way?'

'I'm known around here as Zack Clay.'

'All right then, Zack, will you take me out to see your land at Bowleg Creek?'

He frowned slightly. 'I could. You know I ran off Tillerman and Ransome, but I'm not sure that those *hombres*'ll stay outta my hair. I don't want to leave the town unprotected in case they come back looking for trouble.'

'All right, give me directions. I can hire a horse and find my own way to Bowleg Creek.'

He looked uncertain, then nodded. 'Yeah, I guess so. I'll take you down to the livery, and give you a note for Will Chess, one of the men working for me.'

On the landing, she opened a small telescopic parasol that he had noticed she was carrying. He was about to remark on it — it was the first he had seen, though there had been talk of their popularity — when he noticed several men running down the street.

Tensing, he turned and shaded his eyes.

Two riders were coming in from the valley trail. No, only one rider. He was leading a horse with what looked like a body draped over it.

He jumped down as she stared, then he began to run towards the gathering crowd. Penny called after him:

'What is it? What's wrong?'

Without turning he shouted back:

'That's Will Chess on the horse, and the other one is wearing Frank Marney's shirt.'

She caught her breath as he sprinted on towards the newcomers. Even from here she could see that Chess could barely sit the saddle, had a bandanna wrapped around his head, and one arm was hanging loosely. His body was tilted all to one side, his face was streaked with blood. He was obviously hurt, and now she could make out large blood-stains on the shirt of the man draped over the second horse. Zack had called him 'Frank'.

She caught her breath, putting a gloved hand swiftly to her mouth.

The signs were unmistakable, even to her unpractised eye: there must have been some truly serious trouble out at Bowleg Creek.

★ ★ ★

Doctor O'Brien looked soberly at Zack as he washed his hands and forearms in a bowl of blood-tinged water. Zack handed him the towel.

'It'll be touch and go with both of them, Zack.'

The marshal swore softly under his breath; Frank was a family man, had been profuse in his thanks to Zack for giving him the chance to earn extra money at Bowleg Creek. He already had three children, all close in age, and his wife was work-worn trying to raise them. The few extra dollars would pay an Indian girl to help with the family washing and other chores.

'Frank's taken the worst beating.' O'Brien shook his head mournfuly. 'Bad, very bad, Zack. So many broken bones. Organs damaged, massive blood loss.'

'Boot work.'

The medic nodded in silent agreement. 'Deep bruises on his arms where I'd say he had been held while someone else administered the beating. As brutal as any I've seen and I used to work the goldfields a few years back. There was always someone being beaten or maimed in an accident.'

Zack was pale, his features were like a death's head, the skin was drawn so tightly over the bone structure. 'How about Will Chess? Can I see him?'

'He'll be coming round soon. Luckily that bullet only creased his scalp, but I had to give him a whiff of chloroform while I set his ribs. More boot work, but the splintered bones never lacerated his lungs, like Frank's. He's got a broken collarbone, too, and almost certainly concussion. He's really in a pretty bad way.' O'Brien paused, took a deep breath. 'Goddamnit, Zack! I've seen men caught in mine cave-ins who weren't so badly injured as these two!'

'It's my fault, Doc. I should've shot those bastards on sight instead of turning 'em loose.'

O'Brien frowned. 'You're talking about Tillerman and Ransome? You can hardly take any blame! You did what you had to do — and thank God you did, Zack, for keeping such creatures out of our town, whether your methods are entirely legal or not! Come into the surgery . . .'

Close up, Will Chess was almost unrecognizable. His face, what could be seen of it between the bandages, plaster strips and sutures, was almost entirely covered by purple-black bruises. His front teeth were shattered, top and bottom lips raw and mangled. His jaw hung lopsided, swollen massively on one side, the eye above having disappeared into puffed flesh. The other eye was barely visible, no white showing, only clotted blood.

'Judas, Doc — where's his nose?' Zack grated.

'Somewhere under all that swelling — he can't breathe through it. That's why his mouth is open. It'll be mighty painful when the chloroform wears off.' He touched Zack's arm, feeling the iron-hard tendons, looked down and saw his hands were balled into fists. 'I think he's coming round now.'

The marshal leaned close. 'Will? You hear me, pard? It's Zack. Who did this? Was it Tillerman and Ransome? Did they go to Hendon's after I run 'em off?'

'Not so much all at once,' admonished the doctor.

It was mighty difficult to make anything intelligible out of the guttural, snorting sounds that came through Chess's bandages, and Zack straightened, his eyes steely.

'What'd he say, Doc? I couldn't make out hardly anything.'

'I've probably had more experience than you interpreting what badly injured men are trying to say, Zack. In essence, Chess said . . . ' He paused; reluctantly, it seemed to the marshal. 'He said it was Tillerman and Ransome. Then — it sounded like, 'Everything's gone'.'

9

War Clouds

The Dutchman was worried about Burt Helidon. He and the Broken H owner had clashed several times over the years, but not too seriously.

They were rivals and maybe encouraged their men to make trouble with the rival ranch crew: brawling, mostly, in town, at least, before Zack Clay took over, but there had never been any shootings or blatant attacks. OK, maybe each had had a few not-so-easy-to-explain stampedes or broken fences but those times had all been settled without gunfire.

Until Dutch Haas got the notion to bring in a couple of fast guns: Lex Bates and Monte Harte. Even then, the shoot-out had been with Marshal Clay, not Helidon's crew.

143

Helidon, of course, saw how things were headed, with Clay falling behind the due date on his Bowleg Creek land. He had sent for Tillerman and Ransome.

And that was what had the Dutchman worried.

He had poached the *pistoleros* from Helidon, and there would be hell to pay over that.

He didn't want a range war, mostly because it might lead to federal intervention, but could be things were heading that way, and if so . . . Well: he'd soon see whether what he was paying Tillerman and Ransome was worth it.

Hank Tillerman looked up from the plate of stew he was eating, warmed over by the surly cook who had been dragged out of his bunk by Gil Jeffries after Dutch had at last decided to make an offer to get the gun-fighters on Windmill's payroll.

They had both been ravenous and ate fast and noisily in the big ranch kitchen while the Dutchman got some money out of the safe; they had agreed to work for Windmill but demanded some cash up front: $250 each.

'Judas priest, I don't keep that much on the ranch!' Haas had complained.

Tillerman shrugged. 'Then I guess we eat an' run. We can still go to Helidon; he pays up front.'

The Dutchman gave in after a while, and before they had finished the meal handed over the cash. Ransome grunted, stuffing the bills and coins into his pockets. Tillerman counted his carefully, glared at Haas.

'Four bucks short.'

'Aw — damn, can't you let me owe you even that much?'

'We work cash on the barrelhead.'

And that was that. Then, after they sat back, each smoking one of Haas's cigars and sipping some of his schnapps they listened while the rancher told them his problems.

'I gotta get that land on Bowleg Creek. I offered to loan Clay some men to help him reach the due date — if he'd agree to sell to me once he had title.' He shook his head, mouth scornful. 'No go. Helidon likely offered him the same deal. But he's too damn stubborn. Took that marshal's job so's he could pay two fellers to finish the prove-up requirements.'

'What've you been doin' about it?' Tillerman asked.

'I just told you! Tried to do a deal with Clay.'

'You ain't doin' much then,' opined Ransome. 'Not if Clay's still pushin' towards his time limit with hired help.'

The Dutchman tightened his lips. 'Look, he outgunned both the men I brought in — '

'Monte Harte was never much: cheap, but slow. Same with Lex Bates. Lotta talk, no action.' Tillerman was scornful of the dead gunfighters. 'You wastin' time, tryin' to stop him your way. What you gotta do is wipe him out.'

Dutch Haas straightened quickly, his

cigar poised halfway to his mouth. 'Whoa! Anythin' like that and the federal marshals'll be down here like a brushfire!'

Tillerman drained his schnapps, studied the glass and wrinkled his nose. 'Not as good as Kentucky bourbon. Look, Dutch, you leave this to us. We'll get Clay off that land once and for all. He'll *have* to quit because there'll be nothin' left for him to work. Even if there was, mebbe he wouldn't be around anyway.'

'Yeah. Look, Dutch, we'll wipe the bastard out,' Ransome tuned in, feeling the effects of the many drinks he had consumed since the meal. He grinned, teeth bared, no humour anywhere to be seen. '*Then* when the son of a bitch comes a'thunderin' out to see what's happened me an' Hank'll be waitin to do our own squarin'-away with him.'

Tillerman nodded but Dutch still looked mighty worried. 'You don't understand. That's government land until such time as Clay proves-up on it.

It's not just territorial gov'ment, but Washington. I don't want no truck with federal law.'

Tillerman smiled crookedly, stopping the next words before they tumbled over the Dutchman's lips.

'That part's easy. We leave sign that points to Helidon bein' to blame. Then you get rid of him, too, and when Bowleg Creek land is put up for settlement again, all you gotta do is be first in line at the land agency.'

Dutch took a few minutes to absorb what Tillerman was saying. When he did his eyes widened and his heart started pounding. His stomach convulsed in a few cartwheels but as the notion settled in it seemed to be a better and better solution.

At last, pouring large drinks all round, he took a deep breath and said,

'Go to it, fellers! Only thing is, what about Chess and Marney? The men he's got workin' for him?'

Hank Tillerman gave him a bleak look.

'It ain't smart to leave witnesses.'

The Dutchman's face slowly changed, the worry lines were back and his stomach tied itself in a knot a Hindu fakir couldn't have unravelled.

★　★　★

They were thorough.

Dutch, watching through field glasses from among the clump of trees on the knoll overlooking Zack Clay's land, felt the sweat prickling his face and running down his chest as Tillerman and Ransome went to work.

They rode in, friendly enough.

Chess was notching logs for the cabin which had two walls completed now; another was halfway finished, with the roof frame mostly in place. They were making damn good progress!

Frank Marney was measuring lengths of wire for the long panel of fencing that would complete the perimeter line.

Both men looked up as Tillerman and Ransome walked their mounts across the creek. The visitors nodded and Tillerman folded his hands on the saddle horn.

'Howdy. Seem to've gotten ourselves lost. Lookin' for Broken H. That you boys?'

'Burt Helidon's place,' Chess said, shaking his head and straightening to ease the kinks out of his back, glad of the interruption. He held the mallet and chisel, whose blade was becoming blunter by the minute, squinting at the strangers. 'You're too far north.' He pointed across the pasture that Frank Marney was fencing. 'Go across that way. Frank hasn't filled in the last section yet. Save you a few miles. When you see a rise with two trees on top and a third, stunted one, on the right, go that way.'

'To the right?' Tillerman asked.

Chess nodded. 'That's it. You'll be on Broken H land in an hour or so and you'll see the big house on top of a knoll.'

'Thanks, *amigo*. You mind we water

our hosses and get a drink?'

Chess made a casual gesture to the creek. 'Hell, no. Long as you don't drink it dry.'

He grinned and Tillerman forced a smile. Ransome merely dismounted, made a production of pressing his hand into the small of his back. He nodded in friendly manner to Frank near by, and Marney said, 'You boys don't look like ranch hands, you don't mind me sayin'.'

'Hell, no,' Ransome said, half-smiling. 'We used to be Texas Rangers. That's where we got that tough look, I guess, but we're really pussy cats.'

Tillerman, dismounted now, said amiably, 'Well, not exactly pussycats. More like mountain lions — with a bellyache.'

They moved concertedly.

Ransome stepped forward, his gun sweeping up and smashing Frank across the side of the head, knocking his hat flying. Then the gun barrel swept back and caught him on the jaw as he fell.

Tillerman didn't even look round.

He saw the startled reaction of Chess as the man dropped the chisel but hefted the hammer. Too slow; Hank Tillerman kicked the log the man was standing on and it rolled just enough to throw Chess off balance. He staggered but made a good try to hit the gunman with the hammer.

But Tillerman moved with the quickness of a snake, dodged to one side, and kicked Chess's legs from under him. Chess sprawled and his left arm flung out. Tillerman moved in that lightning-like way and dropped the log across the arm.

Chess cried aloud in pain as it skidded up to his shoulder and they both heard the collarbone snap. The cowboy passed out and Tillerman swore.

'Dammit! Here, Carey, lemme help you with Marney. We can amuse ourselves with him till Chess comes round.'

★　★　★

Up in the stand of timber, Dutch Haas kept the field glasses pressed tightly into his eye-sockets. Breath hissed between his teeth as he rose slightly in the stirrups.

'Judas priest! I'm sure gonna stay on the right side of those mean bastards!'

Tillerman heaved the barely conscious Frank Marney to his feet, stood behind him, holding him by the upper arms in a tight grip. He nodded to Ransome who spat on his palms, rubbed them together and set his boots firmly as the hands formed into knotted fists. He slammed two rapid blows into Frank's midriff. The man gusted breath, gave a half-cry in his dazed state, and tried to draw up his legs.

Tillerman was braced to take his weight and bared his teeth as he shook the man, forcing him to plant his boots on the ground. Ransome danced around him, thumbing his moist nostrils occasionally, eyes bright and sparkling as he drove home body-jarring blows, smashing them into the midriff, the rib cage, the contorted face which swelled quickly after repeated hammerings. The eyes closed, lips split, teeth loosened. Ransome swore as his split knuckles kept sliding off the bloody flesh. He was breathing heavily and Tillerman had to brace his legs and ram his elbows into his body so as to support Frank's dead weight.

'He's gettin' — too — blamed — heavy!' he gasped.

Ransome's eyes had the look of craziness as he blinked and briefly focused them on his pard.

'Let him drop. My arms're tired, but my legs ain't!'

Tillerman let Frank fall and the man landed half on his side, blood spraying. Ransome stepped in quickly and began kicking the unconsious, badly injured man brutally, scuffing dirt as he moved around him, boots working all the time.

He rounded fast, fists coming up when he felt a hard grip on his shoulder, turning him. His fist was cocked, his face was wild and contorted, flecks of

154

foam frothed at the corners of his mouth
But he had enough sense left to recog-
nize his pard and lowered the fist slowly.
'What?' he gasped.

'That's enough. My turn on Chess.'

For a moment it seemed Carey
Ransome would argue, but then he
wiped stinging sweat from his eyes,
nodded and, chest heaving, went and
sat on a log.

Tillerman moved in on Chess and
began kicking him, walking around the
prone man as Ransome had walked
around Frank Marney. His boots and
the cuffs of his whipcord trousers grew
dark with Chess's blood.

Tillerman, a heavy smoker, was short
of breath and stood back, wiping his
face with a corner of his neckerchief.

'Aah, let me finish for you,' growled
Ransome, trying to push the other asde.

But Tillerman wasn't having any of
that. He thrust his pard back, deliberately drove his boot heel into Chess's
shoulder, making sure the collarbone
was broken. He stumbled and went

down to hands and knees. He came up cussing a blue streak, eyes wild.

'*Goddammit to hell!*' he snarled.

'Come on! Or we'll be here all day! We gotta set the fires yet!'

Tillerman's eyes blazed at the other, then slowly he nodded. 'Hell with the son of a bitch, anyway! I'm too tired to spend much time on him!'

Before Ransome realized what he was doing, Tillerman drew his Colt and fired. Will Chess's head jerked violently and blood flooded across his bruised and battered face.

'Spoilsport!' Ransome said with a sneer. 'OK. See if we can find some coal oil and I'll drag some of this brush against the cabin walls. There won't be much of this place left in an hour or so.'

'Then we wait for Clay to come ridin' in, hell for leather.'

'He might come in that way, but he'll go out a lot slower — in a pine box.'

They grinned at each other: well pleased with their work — and how the remainder of their job was shaping up.

10

The Killing Ground

Zack could smell the wood smoke even before he crossed the ridge and came within sight of his homestead land at Bowleg Creek. A dirty smudge like an anaemic rain-cloud hung in the air above the first bend. It tasted bitter against his tongue when he licked his lips.

He reined in the grey sharply, patting its head apologetically for having used unnecessary force. He half-rose in the stirrups, his face grim as he stared at the charred remains of the log cabin, the smashed and broken fences. Many of the posts were burned, too, and the corrals were wrecked. The small remuda he had gathered was gone, scattered in the hills, no doubt, and the domestic cow he used for milk and keeping the grass down around his campsite lay dead on its side, its legs starting to rise as bloating began in the day's heat. The lean-to was no more than a pile of smouldering ashes.

His tools were gone, except for a few deliberately smashed ones, which had been tossed around. There were many tracks, which didn't necessarily mean there had been many raiders.

Two or three riding back and forth in an orgy of destruction would leave such a jumble, and the remuda would have left tracks as it was driven off. There was nothing in these overlaid hoofprints for him, but, afoot and carrying his rifle, he worked his way out, past the smouldering logs and wrecked cabin foundations. He found where the tracks became less congested, branching eventually into three separate trails. So, at least three riders had caused the destruction, he thought grimly; he figured he knew who two of them were. On closer examination he decided the third set of tracks had been made by the same horse as on one of the other trails. The rider had doubled back, laid this false trail.

A feeble attempt to confuse him. So it was down two raiders again. *Bueno!* Had to be Tillerman and Ransome.

He stood there in the midst of the wreckage of his dreams, strangely feeling little at first. Then his fingers began to ache as they gradually tightened their grip on his rifle. He felt blood roaring in his head; breath hissed through distended nostrils and a murderous fury surged within him. His friends had been brutally beaten, both of them very likely fatally, then everything he had built had been systematically destroyed. So it was finished — dream ended.

That was the thought that whipped through his aching brain. *Ended*. He could never meet the time limit now — well, possibly with a huge team of men working long hours, but that was not going to happen so wasn't even worth thinking about.

So. It was back to the old time, the time when the feelings and reactions he had tried to bury deep within him, for Lucy's sake, exploded to the surface again, demanding release. Even as these thoughts formed, he propped his rifle against a smoke-blackened rock and took out his six-gun, checking the loads, testing the action, before dropping it back into leather.

Yeah, this was how it was going to be. He had left his badge in Benbow; this chore only required a gun, not a brass star which had no meaning out here anyway.

He was going man-hunting once again, and if necessary dead men would stretch behind him, like a mile of railroad ties, until he had settled this — his way.

*　　*　　*

When he reached the knoll called Two-and-a-Bit — two tall trees and a stunted one — he saw that the raiders had been met by a third man. The tracks the newcomer left were distinct from the others: his horsehoes had a Broken H moulded into the bend, with a small notch on either side of the 'H'.

He knew these were Helidon's 'special' shoes, which he had fitted to the top-quality horses he broke in, personally trained, and sold all over Colorado and New Mexico, with a promising market building well in Louisana, up around Beauregard and de Quincy. These animals were progeny of the small group of genuine Arab breeding stock that Helidon ran on Broken H. He had almost bankrupted himself bringing them to the US and now they were at last starting to pay off.

The shoes were specially forged by a blacksmith in St Louis, a Hungarian artisan who had once worked in the huge breeding-stud estates outside Vienna, where pampered horses sold for many thousands of dollars. There was something in the man's past that didn't invite investigation, though, and he was not averse to making a few extra dollars by selling 'exclusive' horseshoes and other equipment, which he made for the richer buyers who liked something 'special' and *individual*: rich folk who felt they had to be 'different' at any cost. Some had their initials or monograms worked into the metal.

The Dutchman had seen some of these made-to-order horseshoes one time at the Benbow freight office, spilling from a burst package of through-freight; shoes and cleats tumbled ankle deep on to the floor. The clerk, Ernie Lee, was in a tizzy because there were an unknown number of shoes missing.

'Helidon'll have me hoss-whipped! He's been waitin' on this shipment.'

'What happened?' the Dutchman had asked.

'Aw, package was on the Lawton Creek run and the wagon toppled into the river after all that rain.' At the time there had been days of rain and part of the trail had collapsed. 'They rescued some shoes, but didn't get 'em all.'

'Well who the hell knows how many's missin'?' Haas pointed out, fingering one of the shoes, running his big horny thumb over the raised 'H' with its broken crossbar. 'I mean, if a set or two went missing from here, how would anyone know that they hadn't been lost in the river?'

It took another twenty minutes before the clerk decided he could use some extra money; when the Dutchman left he carried away a set of the shoes in the bottom of his warbag. *Just never know when I might have a use for these*, he told himself, riding back to Windmill.

And now he had finally found that use: leaving an unmistakable trail pointing towards Broken H from the ruins of Zack Clay's quarter-section. An accusing finger . . .

'Thought they was special shoes Helidon fitted to them expensive Ay-rab bosses he breeds?' said Tillerman, as he watched a ranch hand fit the shoes to

Haas's big black horse. The Dutchman winked.

'He rides an Ay-rab himself, with these sort of shoes. The hoofprints'll put him right here on the spot.'

Tillerman nodded, almost smiling, but Ransome frowned. 'A dozen of his ranch hands'll swear he was nowhere near Bowleg Creek!'

'Won't matter. We lay these tracks especially for Zack Clay to follow — and they'll point him to Helidon.' Haas shrugged. 'Who knows what'll happen then?'

'Yeah, could work. But Clay won't get as far as Broken H,' Tillerman said, grimly.

The Dutchman spread his hands. 'Well, there you are. The shoes are just a decoy any way you look at it.'

★ ★ ★

Entirely unaware of this conversation, of course, Zack dismounted and examined the tracks that meandered down the far slope of the rise. In the distance he could see Broken H's boundary, a few grazing cattle, the smoke of a branding fire with a group of cowboys moving around it, even hear the faint bawl of the cattle as the iron burned the brand into their hides.

He followed the trail downslope and through a cutting that swung away from Broken H to a narrow part of Bowleg Creek, well beyond his own land.

Zack stopped, rifle still in hand, and paused briefly, then suddenly he jumped the grey between two boulders.

Too damn convenient, this trail! Too easy . . . .

At the same time a rifle cracked and lead laid a spurting line of dust across the lichen-scabbed rock, inches from his head. He ducked and the horse whinnied and plunged as chips of rock stung its neck.

Zack went sideways out of the saddle, hitting hard and raising a cloud of dust. Belly down, almost breathless from the drop out of the saddle, he rolled in against a low rock. Bullets were searching for him, lifting a storm of grit in a ragged line.

He used this screen as he threw himself over the low rock, back-sliding, and scrabbling under a deadfall. He was pretty sure the gunman couldn't see him.

Bullets slammed into the low rock where the ambusher had last seen Zack, then screamed away. His horse whinnied and shrilled, but had enough sense to work its way deeper in amongst the big boulders.

Zack spotted the man's position, high up the side of the cutting, behind a thick bush that slanted out at an angle. He raked it with a swift, thundering volley of four shots. Twigs exploded from the bush, leaves were cut adrift. The man lurched upright briefly, and Zack recognized Carey Ransome before he dropped back. Zack put two more shots into the bush, shaking it violently, but he didn't glimpse Ransome again. Nor did the man shoot back.

But Zack had given away his own

position and he realized, too late, that part of Ransome's job had been to draw his fire; he might have been wounded doing it, but the killer had been successful.

Zack found that out when something seared across his back, drove him face first into the deadfall. His nose started to bleed and his head buzzed. He spat out some moss from the log, even as he instinctively rolled into the hollow beneath. A volley of six hammering shots raked the deadfall. He winced, cringing away from spinning stone chips and thrumming splinters. The lead came whistling in from above but well to the right of his cover.

Tillerman was lying in wait. They had set it up, let Chess take the critically injured Frank into town. Clay would know immediately what had happened at Bowleg Creek, and hell or high water wouldn't keep him from coming after them. Then they had simply waited, faked a trail towards Broken H to bring him here, to the killing ground.

Or maybe the trail hadn't been faked; maybe it was genuine, and whoever had been riding the mount with the special shoes had gone on ahead, leaving Tillerman and Ransome to take care of Zack Clay.

And they had damn well come close to doing just that! He was beginning to feel the wound in his back as the first numbing effects faded; pain was spreading so that he couldn't tell just where the lead had hit him. He thought — hoped — that it had only creased him, but the flesh was so thin there that the shoulder blade would be damaged in some way. Waves of dizziness now blurred his vision, and deep breaths hurt. He tightened his grip on the rifle but it didn't feel as positive as it should. His left hand had lost some of its strength and feeling. He couldn't afford to pass out!

Do that and he would never wake up.

Tillerman raked the deadfall again and a slug came close enough to hit the heel of one boot, twisting Zack's ankle painfully with the impact. It had been a glancing blow and the heel was still in place, though with a new groove across it, deep enough to lay his little finger in.

He backed up as much as he could, grunting with the effort and pain that shot through his shoulders like a hundred knives pricking him. If they pinned him down — and they *could* from their positions — he wouldn't have a chance. They could pick him off at their leisure.

Blood had reached the small of his back now, pooling against his trouser belt. He gasped involuntarily as he moved, feeling the sharp pain on the inside edge of his left shoulder blade: *splintered or chipped bone?*

He wasn't going to be able to use his rifle to its full potential; his left hand couldn't be trusted to grip the fore end firmly. Resting it on the deadfall and shooting one-handed wouldn't be accurate without the barrel's being held steady. He let the Winchester fall, pushing it back under the deadfall; no sense in leaving it as a target to be destroyed by Tillerman's pot-shotting.

He palmed up the six-gun, and when Tillerman had finished with his next volley he put two slugs through the middle of the billows of gunsmoke. There was no immediate result but, as he struggled to stay conscious, there was violent motion up there and Hank Tillerman fell forward, grasping wildly for something to keep him from tumbling downslope.

He missed whatever he was trying for and came rolling and crashing down the steep side of the cutting, on his back, trying desperately to brake his slide. Dust rose thickly and, teeth gritted, Zack bellied out, got to his knees and laid the Colt across the heavy log.

Tillerman skidded and slid the last few feet, lay still for only an instant and, being the professional he was, forced movement into his limbs, desperate to get under cover. Hatless, he looked wildly towards Zack's position, saw the steady Colt tracking his movements and, with a roar, he lurched to his feet, drawing his own six-gun with a surprisingly smooth and swift motion, considering the tumble he had just taken.

Their guns roared together. Tillerman's lead chewed a line of flying splinters out of the deadwood. Zack fired again and Tillerman's legs went all askew. His body weaved and he bent almost double in his efforts to stay on his feet; his face contorted with the effort of trying to straighten and bring up the Colt.

Zack shot him high in the chest. That straightened him, violently, hurling him back a yard; then his boots tangled and he sprawled, half on his side. He flopped on to his face and was still; maybe there had been one searing moment of surprise an instant before his brain ceased to register anything. But it just might have recorded that he had made a mighty good effort with his last fast draw. Just not good enough.

Zack rolled half on to his right side, fumbling with his tingling left hand to press the used shells out of the Colt's cylinder. He replaced them with fresh cartridges from his belt loops, using his right hand — these fingers were faster, more competent — the gun resting in his cupped left hand.

He waited, belly-down again, well protected behind his log, willing himself to stay fully conscious, searching for Ransome.

Minutes passed. How many he couldn't tell, but he didn't relax, still fighting his body's urge to give in to temporary oblivion, and allow time for recovery. He couldn't afford even one second's black-out . . .

But Carey Ransome didn't come.

Through the increasing roaring in his ears, Zack heard the clatter of hoofs fading away at the far end of the cutting.

Slowly, he rested his forehead across his bent right arm on the deadfall. Maybe if he stayed still for a while, the pain of his wound would ease.

And then he could continue his manhunt.

There could be — *would* be — no

rest until Carey Ransome was dead by his hand.

No rest.

★ ★ ★

'By Godfrey! That's the last straw!' exclaimed Judge Granville, his mutton-chop whiskers fairly standing straight out from his jowls. His rheumy eyes rolled once and then settled as he looked at Con Magee from the general store and Lin Cadell from the livery. 'You're certain?'

Cadell, who was sweating and still had a quirt attached to his right wrist, nodded. He was a solid man, thick-wristed, with legs like young trees.

'My man and me were on the way to the Sands' place. Old Jeremiah's finally decided to sell me those two old buggy rigs I've been after for years. They were used by General Starke and his staff when he went to sign the armistice ten days after Appomattox. Lot of history wrapped up in those vee-hickles and . . .'

The judge made an exasperated motion. 'Lin, did you or did you not sight a trail herd?'

Cadell nodded firmly. 'Already said I did. Was Ted Purvis spotted 'em first, give him the credit. It's headed this way, Royce, and Zack Clay's off tendin' to his own business.'

'Mebbe he'll be back before they get here,' Magee said hopefully, always a man who would head off trouble if he could. But he saw the cloud darken the judge's face and held his peace.

'Might be back, might be not! What difference does it make? We hired Clay to keep this town law-abiding — '

'Well, he's done pretty good so far, Royce.'

Granville glared at Magee. 'Up to a point. I mean, we had to have a shoot-out, a street brawl and a minor riot before he got things settled down, but I guess that's acceptable. *Has* to be!'

'Gotta admit he's kept it nice an' peaceful since, Royce,' allowed Cadell. 'Be fair.'

The judge grunted reluctant agreement. 'It's not his past performance we're dealing with now! He's — not — here! He can't perform at all, and we have a trail herd on our doorstep!' He shook his large head. 'You know what these hell-raising trail crews are like! No law around, so they'll run riot. And,' he glared at the other two, 'I don't mind adding, some of our stores, and certainly our saloon, will flout the town ordinance and trade all through the night! Just to keep the dollars rolling in! This town'll have the lid blown off it, be labelled 'wide-open', unless by some miracle, Clay returns in time.'

Lin Cadell sighed. 'I sent Purvis to have a closer look. He reckons they could be here by sundown.'

'Not today?' the judge asked quickly.

'Today. They're just south of Windmills west line already. They'll likely rest the herd on the flats out of town, leave half the crew to guard 'em while the rest ride in. Some trail bosses do that.'

'Then let's hope *this* trail boss treats

his men that well, and that we only have *half* a trail crew to deal with!'

'Purvis says he thinks it's Blackjack Tom again.'

Magee frowned. 'So soon? Be a mighty fast turnaround if it is.'

'Well, Purvis ought to know. He worked for Blackjack before he come to me.'

All three looked at each other, the faintest glimmer of hope behind their worried eyes.

'If it is Blackjack, well, he took a shine to Clay before; took his men in hand, too, and. they behaved themselves tolerably well. We just might get through this after all. No thanks to Zack Clay!' Then the judge's voice and face hardened. 'I started to worry about him as soon as he stopped the stage and took those two so-called gunfighters off somewhere. I admit, keeping them from town is fine, but it's way beyond his authority and as a member of the judiciary, I'm responsible for hiring him. So, as far as I'm concerned, this time he's finished: for not doing his job, running off to tend to business of his own. Are we agreed? I know he's had a hard time, but he took our money so he's obligated to look after the town first.'

They all turned as one as the door opened, letting sunlight into the dim room at the back of the store.

Penny Hatton stood there, tapping her collapsible sunshade against one leg, her lovely face now severe.

'Forgive my intrusion, gentlemen — and I use the term quite loosely . . .' She ignored their surprised mutterings. 'I've been waiting outside that door because I wish to see Mr Magee, about supplying him with some fine fabrics from my chain of stores. I couldn't help overhearing part of your discussion.'

'You were eavesdropping, you mean!' snapped the judge, but Penny merely shook her carefully coiffured head, topped by a hat of a quality never before seen on the streets of Benbow.

'You ought to be ashamed of

yourselves! Zack Clay's a man who did his best for you, alone, don't forget. No backing from even one person in this town! Now his back's to the wall and he's lost everything. Not only his livelihood but his two best friends Will Chess and Frank Marney; they died within an hour of each other.' Her cool gaze raked the now shocked and uncomfortable trio. 'Zack has gone to hunt down their killers. You ought to be thankful that he has; he'll keep those particular men from entering town if he has his way.'

'Yes! 'If he has his way!' ' snapped the grumpy judge. 'He might not apprehend them! If he's hurt — or killed — they'll be free to come to Benbow whenever they want! And we'll have no protection!'

'I hope you're wrong, Judge! But if not — well, you can hardly accuse Zack of not doing his duty. You'll just have to call the citizens together to form their own protection group. Take some responsibility for keeping law and order in their own town.'

'Woman, we hired Zack Clay to protect us and the way I see it, it's *his* responsibility. Now, you're a stranger here, and I would consider it a favour if, in future, you do not barge in unannounced when we are in the midst of an official town committee meeting. So we bid you good day!'

'I've already explained how I came to be here.' Penny gave him a smile that was as good and as effective as a slap across the judge's bewhiskered face. 'I'm leaving, Judge, and gladly. But you might like to know that the herd that's coming belongs to me.'

That shook all three of the men.

'I am Zack's wife's cousin, and I have an interest in his welfare. He treated her very well while she lived, and he honours her memory by trying to build a kind of memorial to her at Bowleg Creek. It was her father, by the way, who first discovered Bigelow Valley. But that's beside the point. I ordered this small herd, some hundred steers, to

179

help stock Zack's land before I knew of all the problems he was having. Fortunately, it is Blackjack Tom who is the trail boss, and he not only treats his men as human beings, but he is punctual. So, there *will* be trail riders arriving in this town tonight. Just how many, I cannot say, but I'll ride out and meet the herd, and ask Blackjack to see that his crew behaves.'

At the door she paused and looked at them over one shoulder as they digested her angry words. 'Whether that will help remains to be seen. Good day — er — gentlemen.'

11

Manhunt — 1

Carey Ransome knew he was at a disadvantage, and not only because of Zack Clay's bullet that he carried just under the skin covering his lower left ribs.

It could easily be cut out — not without some pain, but Ransome had scars from other, more serious bullet wounds and knew he could stand it. Still, he didn't want to take the time now. He would have to sterilize the knife blade, which meant fire of some kind, then he would have to steel himself for the first cut — a natural hesitation — and if the lead slug didn't fall out, it would mean probing, and that would break out the sweat . . .

'Take too blamed long!' he gasped, gritting his teeth as pain knifed through

181

him when the horse jarred down the steep incline. 'Gotta put as many miles as I can between Clay and myself. Never figured Hank would go down to the sonuver!'

Sweat stung his eyes and he wiped a hand irritably across his brow, shaking his head. He had wadded a kerchief over the wound but it was sodden with blood already and he knew he was going to *have* to stop long enough to get a spare shirt out of his warbag, tear it into bandages, and bind the wound tightly enough to stop the bleeding.

Be one helluva way to go, weak from blood loss, and have Clay ride in on him!

The other disadvantage — and a big one — was that he didn't know this country. Sure, the Dutchman had brought out all his maps and marked the best escape routes in red, but Ransome had never been all that good at reading maps or finding landmarks; Tillerman had been the navigator.

Looking around now, trying to ignore

the headache and throbbing pain in his side, he wasn't even sure whether he was in the small canyon they had planned to be as part of the escape route; they all tended to look alike to him.

Dammit, the Dutchman should've waited somewhere to make sure they got away safely. 'Course, none of them had expected Tillerman to be killed . . .

'Ah! At last!'

He spoke aloud, standing in the stirrups, for the moment ignoring the pain it cost him. He had just glimpsed water through the brush below and he knew it was the lower Bowleg; if he followed it he would eventually come to Windmill.

Cursing with the twisting and turning, he urged his mount down the steep trail, started through the brush and splashed into the brown, sluggish water.

The horse was maybe halfway across when Ransome noticed a few dead leaves drifting past on his left. His *left*!

That was when he felt the hollow

twisting in his bowels, a sudden, sour taste in the back of his throat.

There was little current here, but — it was going the wrong way!

Actually, there was nothing wrong with the current; it had to follow the flow of the creek. And it was taking the dead leaves sluggishly downstream, which was natural. But Ransome had approached from the wrong side; he realized that not only was he upstream from Windmill, but that he had entered the wrong canyon and could even be heading back towards Zack Clay's land!

Dammit! He was lost.

And in more ways than one, for he glanced back up at the heights he had descended and caught a vague movement up there through sparse timber.

It resolved itself into a horseman, leaning from the saddle on a big buckskin gelding as he studied the trail. Clay forked a horse exactly like that! As he straightened up, Ransome saw that he was holding a rifle across his thighs.

And he was already well within range.

Morrie Clegg quit the saddle of his racing bronc and let it skid in a spurt of flying gravel. He had to run at a fast clip, stumbled, almost fell, putting down a quick hand to keep from biting the dust.

Burt Helidon was just fixing his new cinch strap to his saddle, which was draped over a corral rail. He looked up sourly and frowned when he saw Clegg staggering in like he was at the end of a four-day drunk; the man's mouth was working, but no words came spilling out as he grabbed at the rails to steady himself, fighting for breath.

Three cowboys who had been working on a new gate for the tick-dip chute scattered as the *segundo's* horse flailed in amongst them before it skidded to a halt, blowing hard and caked with a thin coating of foam.

'Judas priest! You sit on a hot brandin'-iron or somethin', Morrie!' one man yelled, the others just glared.

Clegg was hanging with one arm over the corral rail, trying to communicate with the now apprehensive Helidon, but he was still too short of breath.

'The hell's wrong, Morrie? You find out what all that smoke was over at Bowleg Creek?' Helidon demanded.

Clegg nodded, swallowing. 'Wasn't . . . Clay burnin' brush as we thought. Was them gunfighters that went to work for the Dutchman.'

Helidon stiffened. 'What were those treacherous bastards up to?'

'Beat the hell outta Chess an' Frank Marney, set 'em ridin' . . . towards town. Never seen me up on the ridge but . . . I wasn't quite . . . game to take a shot at 'em. Then they wrecked everythin'. Set fire to it all.'

'What? Clay's cabin . . . and the lean-to?'

'The lot. Burned it all to ashes, run off his remuda, shot his milk cow.'

Helidon blinked, then smiled. 'Why didn't I think of that!' Actually he had, but had dismissed it as a bad idea at the last moment; he knew it could become a federal issue, which meant US marshals being called in. No one in his right mind wanted to tangle with them. 'Be kinda nice if we could prove they was followin' the Dutchman's orders; that'd get him outta my hair!'

'Dutch was there, boss.' Helidon froze, frowning, staring in disbelief. 'Back a'ways, just watchin' at first. Then he started layin' a trail right below me on the ridge. When he'd finished, he rode back towards Windmill, leavin' Tillerman and Ransome.'

Helidon nodded slowly. 'I get it. When Clay found out from Chess what had happened he'd come a'smokin' — and they'd be waitin'.'

'That's what happened. But Clay nailed Tillerman and Ransome lit out. Clay's been hit in the back by the looks of him but he's still goin' after Ransome. I think *he's* winged, too.'

'While Dutch sits at home swillin' his goddamn schnapps! Mr Innocent!'

Clegg had settled down enough by

now to roll and light a cigarette. 'Boss, I got a good look at them tracks the Dutchman was layin'. They been made with some of your special hosshoes, the ones with Broken H embossed on 'em.'

'The hell you say!' Helidon roared. 'How — where — goddammit! What's Dutch doin' with my special shoes?'

'Dunno how he got 'em, but he laid the trail pointin' right towards Broken H.'

'*Son of a bitch!*'

Then Helidon went very still, staring fixedly ahead, but Clegg figured he wasn't seeing him or the corrals or anything else on Broken H.

He was seeing Dutch Haas, likely swinging from a lynch rope.

Very quietly, the rancher said, 'Get the men.'

★   ★   ★

Zack was certain sure that Ransome must have seen him.

Because of the wound across his left

shoulder blade the strain of leaning down from the saddle to check the trail made him gasp with pain. He went to straighten, fumbled and almost fell. But his wild grab for the horn and the swing of the rifle he held in his right hand set the brush swaying.

Ransome would have to be blind not to have noticed.

But the killer had spurred his mount through the creek and up the far bank, lashing with the rein ends, raking with his rowels, heading for the cover of rocky slopes beyond.

Zack settled firmly in the saddle again, threw the rifle to his shoulder, but he was too slow; that left arm and shoulder were stiffening up and they let him down.

Ransome ran his mount in behind some half-buried boulders, scabbed with lichen and even a little greenery sprouting from soil caught in the cracks. Zack held his rifle, silently cursing the restricted movement of his shoulder.

Since the war he had carried in his warbag a square of polished steel used for signalling waiting troops when he had been scouting ahead or working behind enemy lines. It was not a perfect surface by any means: rippled and distorting, but its main function was to catch the sunlight, flash a signal to the rest of the soldiers; it was perfect for that.

He had propped it on a rock and stripped to the waist. By a series of painful contortions he managed to see the wound in his shoulder, a little at a time. The wound slanted left to right, a shallow furrow made by a down-driving slug, which could easily have killed him if Tillerman's aim had been just a mite better. A small, clean white area told him the shoulder blade had been exposed and this was most likely the seat of all his pain, the slug no doubt having torn nerves and ripped through a layer of muscle. He washed it by awkwardly pouring canteen water over his shoulder and allowing it to slide down his back. Then he tore his spare shirt into strips and a few squares, wadded the latter over the wet skin, but made a mess of wrapping the strips around him. They were in place, but too loose and kept sliding off. In the end, he took his rope from the saddle horn and worked several coils under his arms, up and over his left shoulder, finally wrapping it around his chest.

It was damned awkward and constricted his breathing a little, but he would get used to it; and it did supply some support to the wounded area and controlled the bleeding.

But it wasn't long before he felt blood starting to ooze again as he climbed down from his mount among the sparse timber, searching for the place where Ransome had gone to ground.

The killer had dismounted. His horse, probably earning a string of blistering curses, showed itself, riderless, between two boulders, then disappeared behind the biggest. It was still saddled, so it could well be carrying Ransome's spare ammunition in the saddle-bags.

Despite the pain and discomfort, Clay smiled thinly. *Say your prayers, Ransome* . . .

There was only one place the killer could be hiding now, crouching behind two boulders about as tall as a man, and as big around as a couple of beer kegs. He would have a good view of the slope where Clay was, but Zack didn't aim to stay put. He ground-hitched the buckskin on a meagre patch of grass and, as the animal lowered its head to investigate, moved behind it and started across the slope.

He had to crouch, and he pushed his hat down his back where it hung by the tie-thong. It wasn't the most comfortable position and in the end he buttoned his left forearm inside his shirt. With this support the pain eased, though he felt off balance, with only one arm to swing, still holding the rifle.

He climbed up about ten or twelve feet and this extra height let him look down on where he figured Ransome had to be. Yeah! There was the man's hat and — *it was swinging this way, the brim rising!* Ransome had already seen him. The gunfighter brought his rifle around quickly and blasted three hammering shots. Two of the bullets whined off the rock beside Zack, and the third went high, *thunking* into a slim tree trunk. Bark sprayed and Zack instinctively hunkered down lower — and saved his life. For Ransome's next shot passed over his crouching form with barely two inches to spare.

Zack withdrew his troublesome left arm from his shirt and felt steadier right away. He grabbed the rough surface of the boulder and thrust his body down into a crevice. The rifle came up and he dropped it neatly into a fissure between the rocks, firming it up, so that the strain didn't need to be taken by his weak arm.

Zack wasted no time, he sighted on Ransome's hat, which was still all he could see of the man, and triggered. The first shot whanged off the rock with a stinging spray of dust and chips but the second passed through the crown of the hat and sent it spinning.

Ransome reacted instinctively, made a snatch at it, rising a little as he did, inadvertently exposing half his upper body. Zack's third shot hit him, either in the left shoulder or a little lower. Ransome fell with a clatter that was easily audible to Clay. The man's rifle slipped between the sheltering rocks, struck another, smaller rock below, and spun away downslope, well out of Ransome's reach — if he was in any shape to try to recover the weapon.

Zack waited, finger on the trigger; the cheekpiece was warm against the right side of his face, the brass curve of the butt was firmly and comfortably snugged into his shouldler.

Ransome didn't appear, but when Zack squinted he could see one of the man's boots jammed between two rocks, heard the gritted curses.

'Dammit! Come — *loose* — you son of a — bitch!'

Uncomfortable crouching, Zack stood slowly, still sighting down his rifle barrel. At the same moment he saw that the boot was empty, deliberately jammed there by Ransome to distract him. The man was play-acting, drawing Zack's attention, while he . . .

Out of the corner of his right eye, Zack saw a slight movement on the periphery of his vision.

He didn't have time to crouch again, so he did the only thing left to him: he let himself fall backwards over the rocks, luckily landing on clear ground, taking the weight on his right shoulder. Even so, the jar of the impact brought a thin red veil down behind his eyes.

Ransome triggered his Colt, the heavy, slapping shots sounding duller than the rifle's.

Clay didn't stay to see or hear where they went. He was behind the boulders now and, gritting his teeth against the almost cramping pain in his upper left side, he ran to get in position above Ransome. He slipped, crashing against a rock. It jarred the rifle from his hand and threw his body outward, exposing him to the killer.

Ransome's face was covered in dirt and some streaked dried blood; his tight, cold smile showed up against this grimy background, wide and eager, as he swept up his Colt.

Sprawled on his back, Clay instinctively rolled on to his left side so as to give his gun arm freedom to move. He didn't even feel the excruciating pain in his chest or shoulders, his mind focused on getting his gun free.

The Colt bucked twice and Ransome's ugly face disappeared in a pulpy mask of blood and shattered bone as the lead knocked him clear over the rock behind him. He toppled off and landed in a huddled heap.

Zack lay there, grimacing now as the pain reached his brain. He fumbled the smoking gun back into the holster, grasped his left shoulder with his right hand and tried to make the whirling earth stay still.

It still felt as if it was heaving beneath him, even when he sprawled on it, face down.

* * *

Burt Helidon and his Broken H crew, on their way to Windmill, heard the shooting.

The rancher had selected the most mean-tempered and ruthless of his hard-case crew, men who would do anything for a few extra dollars in their pay packet, no questions asked.

He had insisted that Morrie Clegg ride with him but the *segundo* wanted no part of his boss's plans. Truth was, he had a sneaking liking for Zack Clay — well, maybe not so much a 'liking' as a form of compassion. No one in the valley knew much about Clay but reading between the lines and picking up on trail talk over the months the man had been here, Clegg had concluded that Zack had had his share of troubles and grief in the past. Clegg was sympathetic because he'd had his own rough passage. It was just plain ornery luck that Zack had chosen his prove-up quarter-section slap bang between Broken H and Windmill, spreads run by two greedy, arrogant men. Clegg didn't care much for Helidon or the Dutchman, but he needed money, so he stayed in his job as *segundo* on Broken H. Chris Fallon, the foreman, had poor health and was thinking of leaving. Morrie was a cinch to take over, and he could sure use the extra pay. Then he could send for sweet Ellie Carmichael back in Denver, bring her out here and make her his bride. That was one thing about Helidon: he paid well.

Morrie knew there would be some things on this ride he wouldn't want to do and he had tried to avoid coming.

'You come!' the rancher had ordered, making it final. 'You're my witness to what Dutch done. I need you along.'

Morrie felt sick; sure, he would be needed — to give some sort of lawful touch to the inevitable lynching of the Dutchman. Now, swinging in towards the area where the shooting had come from, they arrived in time to see Zack shoot Ransome.

Burt Helidon gave Clegg a cold smile.

'Looks like we clean up everythin' all in the one day!' He gestured to two men riding slightly ahead. 'Mitch, Canada, get down there and bring me that son of a bitch of a town marshal. I want him alive. Well — mostly so will do.'

He winked at the tight-faced Morrie Clegg, who looked away quickly.

'Go an' give a hand, Morrie. You look like you need some exercise to wake you up. You're movin' like an old woman. Anyone'd think you didn't want the extra cash.' He raised his voice slightly, 'Bonus for the man who brings him in.'

The others who hadn't been ordered into the search looked at their boss swiftly, anxiously, and he grinned tightly, jerking his head towards the rocky slope.

'Go on! Might as well make a good job of it.'

The hardcases spurred forward in a ragged line and, Clegg, moving more slowly, knew Zack Clay wouldn't last out the day.

12

Searchers

Zack saw the hunting party string out along the ridge and groaned.

Hell almighty! He was so damn *tired*!

But there would be no rest now, he decided, counting the men. Ten, or was it twelve? Stand still, dammit! What did an accurate count matter, anyway? They were all armed and no doubt being egged on by Helidon, with orders to shoot him on sight.

He was moving, with a lot of effort and not inconsiderable pain, even as he took in his situation. It was clear enough to him: Helidon had learned that the Dutchman had turned Tiller and Ransome loose on Will Chess and Frank Marney, then burned out everything after setting the badly injured men on the trail back to Benbow.

Word would reach Helidon soon enough, but Tillerman and Ransome had planned to be waiting at Bowleg when Zack came a'running. There was no doubt about that happening, nor any doubt that Zack would ride into an ambush.

With Zack dead, the Dutchman would make his move to take over the quarter-section, putting in his own man — young Gil Jefferies or the like.

Burt Helidon wouldn't risk that happening; he wanted that land, even if it remained as it was, a charred shambles. It didn't matter — as long as it was in his name and he had control, which meant control of Bowleg Creck, a clear threat to Dutch Haas. Step out of line and Broken H would cut the water supply to Windmill any time Helidon felt like it . . .

The same would apply in reverse if the Dutchman got his hands on the quarter-section.

So, Helidon would hunt down Zack and kill him. Then ride into Benbow and sign up for prove-up, nominating one of his own men as the new settler.

By now Zack was streaming with sweat, breathing heavily, wishing he had his rifle, though he didn't know if he could have carried an extra five or seven pounds over this rugged country with that weakened arm.

Dust flicked from a rock a foot to his left. He heard the crack of the rifle an instant after seeing the spurt of dust. Then there were other spurts, not close enough to be dangerous, but plenty close enough to tell him the man-hunters were closing fast.

He didn't waste time shooting back, or even pausing long enough to see where they were; he cast just a brief, sweeping glance as he turned his back, spotting several horsemen running their mounts at the base of the boulder-shot slope, too.

His own horse would have been an asset but the animal had likely gone to ground; like most animals when hurt or sick, they preferred to be alone with their problem, hiding out someplace.

His back was sore but the layers of rope had protected the wound to a certain extent from all the rough treatment it had received. Now, if he could thrust the pain to the back of his mind, he might be able to move fast enough to find some cover where he could hide out as effectively as the wounded buckskin.

He stooped over, using hands and driving legs — which were still the most powerful of his limbs — to make progress up the slope. Guns hammered behind. Men yelled. Bullets screamed off boulders, tore lines in the dirt. Once or twice they came close enough for him to feel the hot whip of air as they streaked past.

He couldn't keep up the pace: his head was swimming, ears roaring, heart hammering, throat so dry he was almost choking as he tried to draw deep breaths into his starved lungs. To make it worse, he was on a gravelly slope and he slid back two feet for every foot gained in height.

A losing battle.

So he suddenly struck out *across* the slope, seeing with a tight grin how he had foiled four riders who were spurring and whipping their mounts *up* the steepest slope to his right. It would take them to the lowest sweep of the ridge crown and they could take their time picking him off.

Now they had to try and set their mounts across the slope after him. It was too much of an angle, the gravel was too loose. Two of them went down after the first half-dozen steps, one man screaming as his horse rolled over him. The cries died abruptly, likely as his broken ribs penetrated his heart or lungs.

The other unhorsed man skidded and slid and rolled down, out of control. The remaining two riders hauled rein and eased their mounts back. So, for the moment, that was four men he wouldn't have to worry about.

Then suddenly a man came out from

behind a boulder, not ten yards from him. Zack slipped and fell, half-sitting down as the man came in, rein ends lashing, his spurs ripping bloody flesh from the protesting mount's flanks. He fought the animal with savage curses and a powerful grip, lifted his carbine one-handed and fired at Zack. Clay flung himself downslope, gaining impetus, and the bullet spun stones against his ear, bringing an involuntary grunt.

He flopped over as the rider spun the short-barrelled weapon around an over-sized trigger guard, cycling the action and sliding another shell into the breech. He lifted it to his shoulder, one-handed again, grinning in anticipated triumph as he triggered. Zack fired simultaneously, driving one high heel into the ground. He jarred to a stop, though only briefly, but it was enough for the Broken H rider's bullet to miss. The man had tried to allow for Zack's downward slide and might well have found his target if Clay hadn't managed to stop abruptly for that brief moment.

The rider reared in his stirrups, flinging the carbine to one side, rolling over the horse's rump, to hit the slope in an uncontrolled slide, arms and legs flailing loosely. Zack's own skid began again and he put down a hand, which happened to be his left one. The arm folded beneath him, spilling him over. But the horse had been running towards him and he was within a yard of it when he dug in both heels. His impetus hurled his body upright. His legs added power to his headlong dive and he hit the horse's arched neck, clamping both arms about it. The animal shook its head angrily, shrilling in his ear but he managed to get a leg up and over and yelled aloud as his twisting body was racked with knifing pain.

He almost passed out but managed to get both feet in the stirrups, which were too short — a minor problem right now — and rode up on the fleeing animal's neck. It plunged on and guns hammered, riders converged.

He yanked the reins this way and

that and was mighty glad he was on top of a cow pony, used to such violent changes of direction and unexpected demands.

A man closed with him, bringing up his Colt. Zack fired his own gun beneath his bent arm. The man pitched sideways, just managed to stay in saddle, but he was hunched over and loose-limbed, obviously hit. Zack swerved away, not waiting to see whether the man fell. Two more men were coming in, holding their fire as he deliberately set his mount between them, almost lying along the horse's back now. If they fired, they would likely shoot one another. He wheeled the panting, sweating little roan downslope, but at an angle, glimpsing a large stretch of brush below. He might stand a better chance of throwing them if he could reach it.

The cow pony was stretching out, mane flying, hitting a ridge fast. Too late Zack saw that there was no ground immediately behind it! There was a swirl of earth colours, grey and reddish-yellow, with tufts of green, a long way below and then he was spilling out of the saddle and falling through space.

The gallant little horse shrilled all the way down, tumbling and skittering near the base of the very steep incline: it was close to vertical, though it angled out twenty feet above the base.

The pursuers hauled rein, two men almost repeating Zack's mistake. One man deliberately crashed his mount on to its side, was flung heavily, rolling, coming to rest at the base of a big rock. It was Morrie Clegg, and he lay there, dazed, feeling the throbbing of his forehead where he had grazed the rock. Blood trickled down his face as he sat up, blinking, seeing his horse struggling up, shaken but safe.

The other man had swung aside but his mount was plunging down the slope now with the bit between its teeth; it had had enough of running and weaving across this steep face of the slope and was making its own decisions now.

Other men reined down and Helidon, standing on a rock where he had been watching, started swinging his arm and yelling.

'Go on over on foot! Morrie — you're closest! Get over the ridge and tell me his body's lyin' down below! If it ain't, you find him!'

Clegg moved slowly and a couple of other men dismounted and crossed the lower section of the ridge. One called back that he could see the roan's carcass but no sign of Zack.

'Christ, man! He can't fly! He's gotta be there. Hey, you other men, get down there and scour that slope, pronto! Do it proper — on foot!'

The men obeyed, not liking to leave their mounts and climb over the ridge, clinging to the steep side of the slope, which was full of rain-eroded fissures and holes where rocks had fallen down with the wind that sometimes blew powerfully enough to blast the earth away from their bases.

Morrie Clegg tucked a kerchief

under his hat and hoped it would hold it in place over the bleeding gash on his forehead. His vision was blurred and Helidon was shouting at him again to hurry up.

Morrie swung over the ridge and immediately began to slide, stones and loose earth going out from under him. He snatched at protruding rocks but was a good fifteen feet down before he found one that held and almost wrenched his arm from its socket.

He grunted and held on, clenching his teeth, legs still swinging. His gun had slipped from the holster and was lying there a couple of yards to his left. The other searchers were all below him now, some half-sitting and sliding on their behinds because of the steepness, calling to one another.

None of them seemed to have any success in finding Zack's corpse.

'How you doin', Morrie?' Helidon was standing atop the ridge now, looking down. 'Check that fissure — *there*! The big, jagged one on your right . . .'

'Lemme get my — gun,' Morrie panted. He eased across, afraid he would start to slide on the steep ground. He eased up to the weapon but, as he stretched one arm and reached with the other, his movements set gravel and dirt sliding and a small wave of it pushed the Colt to the very edge of the fissure.

Clegg swore softly and made his way across a few inches at a time. He ignored the impatient yelling of Burt Helidon, saw that his gun had caught on a small ledge just inside the lip of the fissure. If he didn't grab it just right the first time it would tumble all the way in and . . .

He froze, his straining fingers a couple of inches from the gun barrel.

There was movement back there in the fissure's darkness. He heard the scrape as a scuffed boot was drawn up slowly and then his eyes were able to pick out features.

Zack Clay was sprawled in there, clothes dirty and torn, blood streaking his face, his body pushed way back tight into the narrowing space. And there was a cocked six-gun held unsteadily in one hand, pointing right at Morrie Clegg.

'Goddammit, Morrie! You'll fall in there in a minute! Is the son of a bitch there or not?'

Their eyes locked, although Clegg could barely make out Zack's pain-racked features. Zack lifted the pistol an inch, his hand shaking.

'*Morrie*!'

Clegg stared at Zack, then started to back out slowly, calling, 'Nothin' here, boss. Almost lost my gun, had to reach in way back after it. It narrows to nothin'. Too small for anyone to hide in.'

He thought he heard Zack's breath release in a long sigh as he stood awkwardly, blowing dust from his Colt.

'Boss!' called Clegg as Helidon started to turn away angrily. 'How about that patch of brush down there? It comes right up agin the foot of this

213

slope. It's just possible he might've made it in there.'

Helidon looked doubtful. 'He'd be banged up plenty if he slid that far! Look at what it did to the roan.'

'Just a thought,' Clegg said and started gingerly to make his way back. As he did, he thought he heard something.

'*Thanks* . . . '

The other searchers began calling in their lack of success, and Helidon swore and swept an arm around angrily.

'All right, dammit! Get on down there and set that brush afire! If he's made it that far it'll either flush him out or finish him — and, me, I'm in a mood where I don't give a good goddamn either way, long as we find the sonuver. Now get to it!'

13

Valley Guns

The Dutchman stepped out on to the porch, holding a half-empty bottle of schnapps by the neck down at his side. His big nostrils were distended and he came more alert as he saw the smoke he had been sniffing for — how long he wasn't sure, because he had been dozing in his chair, sucking at the bottle every so often, perhaps dreaming about Tillerman and Ransome finishing off that lousy homesteader.

He snickered a little drunkenly, just on the edge. Hardly worth shooting Clay now: there was nothing left for the man here now that Bowleg Creek had been destroyed.

The crew who had been working the home range were gathering in the yard. Ramrod Cal Westerman, a rugged man in his mid-forties, lifted his hat and scratched at his sweat-soaked pepper-and-salt hair. He turned and saw the Dutchman.

'Way over in the north-west pasture, Dutch. We ain't got anyone workin' over there.'

'Be that big patch of sage and sotol, foot of Injun Leap,' offered the wrangler, a wiry, tall streak of misery calling himself Conchas, on account of wearing such items on his belt, the edges of his chaps, his hatband, and, some said, even on his underwear. 'Damn! There's mustangs up in them foothills an' I just found where they water. Was gonna trap some for round-up an' — '

Dutch broke in roughly. 'It ain't been hot enough for a fire to start by itself an' we ain't had any wildfire. Saddle up. We're goin' out there.'

Donny Bancroft, a top hand who had been out rounding up mavericks said, 'Thought I heard shootin' when I was workin' over on the next range a little earlier, boss.'

'The hell didn't you say somethin'?'
It was likely Tillerman and Ransome
finishing off Clay but . . . why the fire?

'I only got back twenty minutes ago,
Dutch,' Donny said with a touch of a
whine in his voice. 'Left a nice bunch of
yearlin's at the brandin' camp before I
come down . . . '

But the Dutchman had swung back
into the house and was reaching for his
gun belt hanging on a nail in the
hallway. He took down his Winchester
from the antler wall-rack, and stuck his
head out through the door again.

'What the hell you standin' round
for! Get your hosses and bring your
guns! *Pronto*!'

★   ★   ★

Zack thought he was going to suffocate,
jammed back in the rock fissure that
was filling with thick scuds of brown-
white, choking smoke.

His eyes were streaming, his nostrils
wet and burning, his lungs unable to

drag down enough clear air.

He thought it had been Morrie Clegg who had backed off without giving him away but couldn't be certain as the man had been silhoutted against the bright sky. He was mighty grateful, whoever it was, but the thing was, he had fallen in here and was now jammed so tightly that he couldn't have got off more than one shot anyway; his gun arm was caught between his right side and the crumbly wall and he wouldn't have been able to manouevre the Colt, maybe not even cock the hammer again.

Not that it mattered now.

He had been struggling to get free of the fissure ever since he had heard Helidon give the order to set fire to the brush. Now the wind had changed, or the fire was making its own air currents as fires usually did when there was a good blaze, and the smoke was filling the imprisoning fissure.

He could barely see the slope now as smoke rolled across and rose in thick billows. The crackling of the brush was loud so he could hear nothing else. Not that Helidon was likely to have men searching this slope now, but Zack would have been happier if he could see or hear what they were doing.

His upper arms were lacerated from the gravelly walls and his efforts to get himself free. Suddenly his right arm slid past the obstruction that was jamming it and he tumbled forward. His head scraped down the wall, and he landed on his knees.

It hurt but he had so many hurts right now that it was hardly noticeable. He recovered the Colt which had fallen from his grip, crawled to the entrance — only a matter of about two feet. He realized how close he must have been to discovery earlier; if Helidon had come across from where he had been sitting his mount, he would have looked straight into the fissure and seen him. *Gracias* again, Morrie — if that's who you were!

Crouching now in the entrance, head

down so his face was only inches above the ground, where the air was clearer, he felt his lungs expand again and, after a brief, passing dizziness, he was able to breathe almost normally.

Smoke billowed but there were clear patches for seconds at a time. He saw that some of the men were mounted, forcing their reluctant horses into the edges of the fire, chasing after it where it had already burnt down. But the ground was covered with hot ash and the horses pranced and whinnied.

As billows rolled and parted to his right, he saw there were men afoot, too, guns in hands, bandannas around their lower faces, following as close as they dared behind the wall of flames. The sun was a blurred white disc as the smoke rose into the hot sky. Shadows were blurred at the edges, red flames consumed them relentlessly.

There was still a lot of brush to burn.

Although he wanted only to lie down somewhere, preferably with cushions under him, Zack knew he had to make the most of the present situation or die.

He had twice glimpsed a bunch of horses down at the base of the steep slope; riders must have made their way down the other side of this place, which he now recognized as Injun Leap, then dismounted and started beating the burning brush in their search for him. The horses would be ground-hitched; he saw some of them tugging frantically at the restraining reins, afraid of the thick smoke and the proximity to the wall of heat and flames.

But Helidon and his men were all facing the other way, and this steep face was covered with billowing smoke more often than not. It would be hard and painful negotiating the steepness, but he had little choice.

After checking the Colt and replacing two empty shells he started out. He had only gone a few yards before he wished he had a neckerchief to tug up over his nose and mouth, but he had used it earlier in an attempt to stanch his bleeding wound. He held the gun in one hand, ready to shoot if he was spotted, but he quickly holstered it. He needed both hands to hold on as he crabbed his way across, boots sliding, fighting for a grip. The strain on his arms was transferred to the torn muscles in his back and he found he was grunting almost every foot of the way.

The smoke enveloped him and he coughed several times; no need to worry about being heard, with the clattering racket and roar of the burning brush effectively blanketing the sound. He kept turning his head to look towards the Broken H crew. None of them was looking behind, urged on by Helidon who was growing angrier by the minute as more and more brush was ravaged and still there was no sign of Zack, dead or alive.

He grew bolder — actually of necessity. He simply couldn't stay crouched and knotted like this, not with the back wound cramping up, his left arm like a piece of lead, without feeling.

It collapsed under him several times and he fell on his face twice.

Zack was going to have to take a chance and slide.

If he could slide to the bottom, then he would be on more or less level ground, could stagger his way to the ground-hitched horses and . . .

No more time to think about it: *do it!*

He figured the backside would be worn out of his trousers as he slid down, using his hands to steady himself — his right one, anyway: once more the left was of little use but he could thrust with it enough to keep his balance. Dust rose in a cloud behind him but was soon lost in the swirling smoke. It stung his eyes again, his head being high enough now to reach the choking scud.

He toppled and rolled the last few yards, skidding under the smoke and coming out into a more or less clear patch. The ground beneath had been burned early in the piece and the fire had moved on, taking most of the smoke covering this area with it. He sneezed seven times, rapidly.

Now there was *too much* smoke-free, or mostly so!

He could see Helidon and two of his men, moving restlessly as they tried to glimpse the edge of the fire as it swept on, leaving smouldering grass and bushes, but no body of Zack Clay. Burt Helidon, impatient as hell, swung around, deciding to grab his mount and ride around the edge of the fire, gun ready in his hand.

He stopped in his tracks as he saw the ragged figure stumbling towards the tethered horses. He shook his head, certain sure he must be seeing things; his Colt was in his holster now. By the time he realized that he was actually looking at Zack Clay the man was in amongst the horses, swinging aboard a high-shouldered chestnut, leaning from the saddle to slap free the reins of the other mounts.

'He's here!' Helidon bellowed, disbelief still edging his voice as he snatched at his six-gun.

Tense with emotion and impatience, he fumbled the draw and by that time the horses were scattering and Zack was spurring away. Helidon yelled again and again, his cries eventually reaching some of his men. They came lumbering up; only two were mounted. By then the Broken H owner was shooting, but he paused to bellow at the riders to get after Clay. They thundered by him, triggering wildly.

The shooting had scattered the freed horses and Helidon threw out his arms, trying to catch one as it snorted and veered away. He almost shot it in anger, but good sense prevailed and he started after it afoot, the other cowboys trying their luck, too.

Zack was lying low along the chestnut's back, twisted around awkwardly; then he saw a rider coming up fast on his left. The man was sliding his rifle from the scabbard when Zack fired. His shot went close and the man rocked dangerously off balance in the saddle, let the rifle fall back into the scabbard and grabbed at the horn.

The second man angled in fast from Zack's right and was lifting his Colt to shoot when Clay saw him, hauled rein with his half-numbed left hand; it was enough to make the chestnut respond instantly, as it did in its normal working day to the signals of its rider. The Broken H ranny's bullet whipped past Zack's face and he jerked to one side, lifted the six-gun and triggered almost in the face of the rider as his mount closed with the chestnut. He slammed back and toppled out of the saddle, his mount racing alongside Zack's.

Bullets whistled around him and he zigagged the chestnut, glanced back and saw three other horsemen coming away from the blaze. Helidon was still afoot but he had a rifle now and he threw it to his shoulder, taking his time beading his target. He fired.

Zack felt the chestnut falter as it whinnied and broke pace. He was jerked about in the saddle, fighting to stay upright and keep the animal going.

Helidon was shooting the rifle fast now, working lever and trigger in a blur, trying to place his lead where his first shot had gone.

But Zack was weaving about now, mostly caused by the staggering of the chestnut as he felt the strength going out of the animal; he had ridden enough wounded mounts in his day to sense that the horse was making its final, desperate run, as hurt animals often did, instinctively putting as much distance between themselves and the source of their pain as possible.

He knew the chestnut was dying but had to take full advantage of its last flight, although he hated to do it; if there had been no danger, he would have stopped and put it out of its misery.

The mount was swaying, slowly, breathing like a huge leaking bellows. The ribcage between his legs expanded and deflated raggedly as he felt the animal going down — and he jumped as it fell and rolled, skidding, crashing into him, knocking him violently along.

As his senses reeled and dulled, he didn't even realize that billows of thick smoke were rolling over him and the downed horse.

The smoke had already blotted out Helidon and his men, caught them napping, blinding them.

Dazed, Zack crawled back to where the horse lay, heaving its last breaths. He threw himself between the twitching legs, hoping the animal had fallen on its right side. Groping with his right hand — he had lost his Colt in the fall — his seeking fingers touched the scabbard on the skewed saddle. Good! Left side uppermost. Holding his breath now, he inched his hand over the edge.

There was a rifle resting in the scuffed leather.

★　★　★

Penny Hatton rode through the dust of the lumbering herd, her fine-quality riding outfit now trail-stained with dust and a few leaves clinging here and there; some were in her hair, too, as her small, narrow-brimmed hat was hanging down between her shoulders by a rawhide thong held with a Spanish silver-and-ivory slide.

Blackjack was out on the left wing, had dropped back from the point earlier. She saw him watching the big smear of smoke rising over the range. He turned as he heard her approach, rode out a'ways from the cattle. They were easy to control, had had good water and grass on the trail, and his men were skilled at their jobs.

'That looks to be a pretty big fire, Blackjack!'

He started to swing his head to the side to spit, then figured he should show better manners. This was a lady of high quality and he felt somewhat in awe of her, though he worked pretty well at hiding the fact; she was also paying his wages, and she was good to work for.

'I figure that could even be on

Windmill land,' he told her, admiring her figure in her dark-green shirt, open at the neck to reveal a tantalizing triangle of pale ivory skin. Her hips filled the grey corduroy britches mighty fine, too . . . He stirred himself.

'Where it drops down to Bowleg,' he added.

Penny stiffened. 'That's where Zack Clay's land is! But — it's hours since it was burned by Tillerman and Ransome.'

'That's grass or brush. Not buildin's.' The trail boss paused, and she saw the tension in his upper body as he snapped his head around. She saw, too, that most of the crew were looking from the smoke pall towards where she sat her horse beside Blackjack Tom.

'What is it?'

Head still cocked slightly on one side, he said, 'Gunfire — an' a lot of it.'

Even as she stiffened and her mouth opened to question him, she heard the distant, ragged tattoo that she would not have recognized as gunfire.

'Is that . . . ? Oh, it has to be very close to Zack's land, Blackjack!'

He was already standing in the stirrups, shouting as he waved an arm. 'There's a pass about a mile ahead. Turn the herd towards it.'

The crew looked surprised but had learned long ago not to waste time when Blackjack Tom had that urgent note in his voice.

'We're makin' a detour and takin' the herd with us!'

Penny frowned as the cowboys swung the cattle in towards the rising hills, the summits cloaked by swirling smoke.

★　★　★

Burt Helidon was going to make this the final assault; he gathered his men around him, all mounted, and was haranguing them in a small, tight group about two or three hundred yards distant from where Clay lay stretched out behind the dead chestnut.

Then Clay lifted his gaze and saw a

231

bigger bunch of riders coming out of the smoke; he had no trouble in recognizing them as riders of Windmill. He tensed, lifted up a little, seeing Helidon's group stirring in alarm.

Dutch Haas led his men. Their guns were out and they started shooting at Helidon's bunch. The Dutchman's bellow reached Zack's cars.

'Got you this time, you trespassin' bastard! What the hell you think you're doin', settin' my land on fire? By hell you done it now, Burt!'

'Wait up!' Helidon bawled. 'We're after Clay! He was hidin' in that brush . . .'

But the Dutchman didn't want to know. The schnapps was warm inside him, firing up his long hatred for Helidon. He could hardly believe his luck in finding the man trespassing and destroying his property! Man, there wasn't a court in the land who wouldn't back up his actions!

And the charges were going to be extreme, because he would never be handed another chance like this.

His men spread out and their guns spoke with authority, shooting to kill, or at least maim.

Two Broken H men at the rear were shot out of their saddles. Clay frowned as he thought one of them was Morrie Clegg, but he was staying out of this for the moment, glad of the respite, only wishing the horse was alive and running with him in the saddle.

There was dust everywhere now, mingling with the drifting smoke, as the riders scattered, every man for himself. Gunfire rattled like someone dropping marbles into an empty drum. Horses whinnied and shied, reared, twisted to bite at their riders' legs in payback for this harsh treatment. Men fumbled to reload in the saddle, the sun that penetrated the pall of dust and smoke glittered briefly on dropped cartridges.

Zack ducked as some riders whipped past and one even lifted his racing mount over his hiding place. He was quickly followed by his pursuer; Zack couldn't tell which man rode for which brand in the mêlée. He pressed into the still warm, dusty hide of the chestnut, rolled on to his side, bringing up the rifle as one man leaned from the saddle, his six-gun swinging down into line. Zack triggered and the man reared back, dropping his gun, clapping a hand to his neck where the bullet had burned across. He swung his mount aside and simply kept on riding, heading into the hills.

Zack had already levered a fresh shell into the breech, hunkered down, alert, ducking as he heard bullets snapping overhead. Several thunked into the horse, lifting dust. Two riders came sweeping in towards Zack, their intentions clear and deadly.

Their guns hammered and he dropped prone between the dead horse's legs. He fired blindly across its body and the nearest rider's mount swerved then, with a shrill whickering, threw the man. He rolled in the dust, came up quickly, bringing up his Colt. Zack, on one knee now, fired, levered, fired again and the man was hurled back by the impact, thudded to the dust and spun twice before going still, on his side, facing Zack.

It was Burt Helidon and he was all through. The second rider had spurred away and was heading for the hills.

It was obvious that the Dutchman's greater numbers were winning. There were bodies, some still, some writhing, all over the ground, riderless horses were running in all directions, choking dust was swirling.

And out of it rode the Dutchman himself, teeth bared, his big rifle angled down as he let his horse prance a few yards from where Zack lay on his side, his left hand once again letting him down: it was numbing up, the fingers clawing, unable to firmly grip the fore-end of the rifle.

The Dutchman laughed briefly, harshly, took his time levering a shell into his breech.

'Well, I'm kinda gettin' used to havin'

to do a job myself if I want it done proper. You're just too damn good, Clay. 'Bout time I got you outta my hair once and for all . . . '

As he spoke there was a rumbling like thunder — but it didn't break and there was no lightning. It went on and on and . . .

'Stampede!' a man bawled, wheeling his mount.

Other riders had been lining up behind the Dutchman but they snapped their heads round towards the narrow pass that cut through the hills and which they used almost every time they needed to go into Benbow.

There were wild-eyed, snorting, saliva-streaming steers charging out of the pass, heading for the riders who were still trading lead further out.

'The hell's this!' yelled the Dutchman, wheeling his mount, rifle held loosely now.

No one was waiting around to see: riders scattered for higher ground, in any direction, leaving the Dutchman alone, his jaw dropping. Then he spun his mount back and brought up the rifle to finish Zack, who was on his feet, unsteady, but upright, swinging his rifle by the muzzle in his good right hand, putting all his weight behind it.

Dutch Haas saw it coming and his eyes widened as he instinctively threw up an arm to protect his head. The brass butt splintered his elbow and he screamed in pain as he toppled from the saddle.

Dutch fell at Zack's feet. Zack brought the rifle butt down squarely between those wide, shocked eyes.

They closed instantly, as the skin split and blood flowed. Then the steers were raging across the battleground, now cleared of both Broken H and Windmill survivors. Zack turned, looking for somewhere to run. Then a horseman came thundering in, and — *no! A horsewoman!*

He couldn't believe it when he recognized Penny Hatton as she put her hired mount, a big sorrel, alongside. He stepped up on to the dead chestnut and slid up behind her.

She spurred away as the stampeding steers thundered past, Zack hanging on with his good arm about her waist.

★ ★ ★

Morrie Clegg had been chest-shot but Doc O'Brien had no doubt that he would survive, the bullet having missed any important organs.

Zack, his left arm in a sling, proper bandages now covering his wounded back, nodded to Clegg where he lay in the iron infirmary bed, looking up at his visitor.

'Owe you, Morrie.'

Pale and drawn with the pain of his wound, Clegg moved his head from side to side on the pillow. His voice was hoarse, not much more than a whisper.

'Was tired of Burt anyway. Too greedy, too — rough.'

They shook hands and Zack said, 'I'm staying on. My — cousin-in-law, I think that's what she is — is financing me to prove up, got a whole crew organized so we'll make it by the due date after all . . . She's gonna buy Helidon's place as soon as the legal eagles release it and learn how to ranch.'

'You gonna be the . . . teacher?'

Zack smiled thinly. 'Might be — if I'm lucky. Listen, I won't be handling the town marshal's job, but Chris Fallon told me before he quit Broken H that you were a deputy in Abilene one time . . . '

'Long time ago — helluva long time ago.'

'Them sort of jobs stay with a man. Chris says you been wantin' to bring a bride out here, but can't quite afford it. I can get you the marshal's job here, when you're better, for a hundred a month. Twice what Helidon was payin'.'

After a minute, Morrie smiled and said, 'Now who owes who?'

'Call it even. We'll have a drink when you're up and about.'

'What happens to the Dutchman?'

'The judge has come out of retirement, acting up big, trying hard for that county appointment. Dutch is in the old powder magazine. Granville says he'll get twenty years in the pen for ordering Tillerman and Ransome to destroy my place. It's still Government property until proved-up, so Dutch is in a heap of trouble under federal law.'

Clegg nodded. 'Won't be so many damn guns in the valley from now on then. Much obliged, Zack.'

'Me, too . . . '

Outside, Penny Hatton was waiting for Zack in a buckboard.

The way she wore that narrow-brimmed hat, canted over the left eye — the smile, where the dimples appeared as well as tiny wrinkles at the outside corners of her eyes . . .

He had to swallow hard: it might have been Lucy holding those reins.

'Climb in, Zack. I've just signed an option on Broken H with Helidon's attorney. He had no kin, no last will and testament. So, pretty soon, you and me are going to be neighbours.'

'Well, neighbour — that's good news.'

'Yes,' she said with satisfaction. 'It is.'

He clambered aboard and as she drove off, he thought: *Neighbours? It might start out that way.*

THE END

We do hope that you have enjoyed reading this large print book.

Did you know that all of our titles are available for purchase?

We publish a wide range of high quality large print books including:
Romances, Mysteries, Classics
General Fiction
Non Fiction and Westerns

Special interest titles available in large print are:
The Little Oxford Dictionary
Music Book, Song Book
Hymn Book, Service Book

Also available from us courtesy of Oxford University Press:
Young Readers' Dictionary
(large print edition)
Young Readers' Thesaurus
(large print edition)

For further information or a free brochure, please contact us at:
Ulverscroft Large Print Books Ltd.,
The Green, Bradgate Road, Anstey,
Leicester, LE7 7FU, England.
Tel: (00 44) **0116 236 4325**
Fax: (00 44) **0116 234 0205**